# DANNY ORLIS
## AND THE
# LIVE-IN TRAGEDY

# DANNY ORLIS
## AND THE
# LIVE-IN TRAGEDY

BERNARD PALMER

*Danny Orlis and the Live-In Tragedy*
© 2024 by Bernard Palmer
All rights reserved. First edition 1970.
Second edition 2024.



Scripture quotations from The Authorized (King James) Version. Rights in the Authorized Version in the United Kingdom are vested in the Crown. Reproduced by permission of the Crown's patentee, Cambridge University Press.

*Cover image: Adobe Firefly*
*Character illustrations: John Ball*
*Editor: Jon D. Fogdall*

Aneko Press *Youth*
www.anekopress.com
Aneko Press, Life Sentence Publishing, and our logos are trademarks of Life Sentence Publishing, Inc.
203 E. Birch Street
P.O. Box 652
Abbotsford, WI 54405

**JUVENILE FICTION / Religious / Christian / Action & Adventure**
Paperback ISBN: 979-8-88936-070-4
eBook ISBN: 979-8-88936-071-1
10  9  8  7  6  5  4  3  2  1
Available where books are sold

# CONTENTS

# CHAPTER 1

# SANDY'S NEW FRIENDSHIP

Brenda Ekberg paused just inside the front door of Fairview Senior High, impatience registering in every movement. She brushed her long, straight hair away from her eyes with a quick gesture and surveyed the almost empty corridor. Sandy Cole was supposed to have waited for her and walked to school with her that morning, but she hadn't.

And Brenda was furious. Waiting for Sandy, or for anyone else, just wasn't her bag. If Sandy wanted to run around with her, she wasn't going to be able to get away with that! She'd have to do what she said she was going to do, or Brenda would be through with her.

She had wanted to see Sandy that morning and find out what her mother had said about the trip to Minneapolis, but it didn't look as though she was going to be able to. Maybe Sandy had a good excuse for not showing up, she reasoned, but it was irritating to have a sophomore pull that on her.

Brenda frowned her indignation. All she had to do was give the word and Sandy would be out. Without Brenda's OK, none of her crowd would have anything to do with Sandy.

The tall, slender high school junior was still standing motionless when a boy with long blond hair hiding his ears and curling up at his shirt collar stopped beside her.

"Hi, Brenda."

She spoke to him curtly without even glancing in his direction. At the moment she didn't want to talk to anyone, especially Steve Bell.

"Hey, what's with you?" he bristled. "You don't have to get so up-tight with me."

A smile softened the lines in her face, but she did not answer him. Maybe Sandy had decided that Brenda and her friends just weren't her bag, and she was trying to avoid them. Or maybe her mother was all shook up because Brenda's skirts were a little shorter than those of the other girls in school. Sandy talked as though her mother didn't care where she went or who she was with, but Brenda wasn't ready to buy that. Sandy was too much of a square to have a mother who was really with it.

She was still thinking about Sandy when Steve put his arm possessively about her shoulder. "Come on, Baby, this isn't our scene. Let's get in my car and split for the day. OK?"

She wriggled away from him. "I've got other things to do."

His lips curled bitterly. "I'll find somebody else."

She shrugged her indifference. "What do you expect me to do? Cry about it?"

At that moment, Alex Smith, the football coach and counselor at Fairview High, came by. Brenda said 'Hi' to him.

Steve eyed her quizzically. "I didn't know you knew him. What gives? Are you going out for football?"

She laughed. "Big joke. Haven't you heard? When your grades get soft, the Establishment provides a 'shrink' for you to talk to–to try and find out your hang-ups."

"Maybe I had better talk to him. I know more about your hang-ups than anyone else."

"Don't you dare! I've got enough trouble already."

* * *

DeeDee Davis hadn't seen much of Sandy Cole either in or out of school the past several weeks. In fact, she hadn't seen much of her since the school year began. It seemed to DeeDee that Sandy and Brenda were together every waking minute. She saw them come into the school building practically every morning.

Usually Brenda was talking, her long, straight

black hair swinging as she jerked her head from one side to the other. And Sandy was usually staring at her with rapt attention. She was letting her hair grow too, the same as her new friend. She had colored her hair the same shade as Brenda's, and she had even begun to walk like her. She was wearing her skirts shorter than DeeDee had ever known her to wear them before, and she sported a wide headband like Brenda's. From a short distance DeeDee had difficulty in telling them apart.

If DeeDee hadn't had to go away for the summer, chances were that Sandy would never have started running around with the older girl. They had met at the laundromat where Sandy and her mother did their washing.

When DeeDee finally got to see Sandy, they had a chance to talk for only a short time.

"You know, Brenda's parents are divorced too," Sandy explained, lowering her voice, "so she understands."

There was something about Sandy's tone that disturbed DeeDee. It was almost as though she was excluded now because her parents were dead instead of divorced. She wanted to blurt out that she understood too, but she didn't. That would only let Sandy know how disturbed she was about the new girl. Instead, she asked her friend to spend the weekend with her.

"Sounds like fun," Sandy replied, "but don't look for me until Saturday night."

"You won't be coming till then?" Disappointment was keen in DeeDee's voice.

"I'm going to spend Friday night with Brenda Ekberg."

DeeDee frowned. That took most of the fun out of it.

* * *

Saturday evening shortly after dark, Sandy came out to the Orlis home to spend the night with DeeDee. She hurried into the house; her young face flushed with excitement.

"Oh, I've had so much fun! Being with Brenda is such a gas!"

Ordinarily Sandy enjoyed lingering in the Orlis living room, talking with Danny and the boys or challenging someone to a game of Monopoly. But on this particular evening she seemed to want to get away from the others as quickly as possible. She hadn't been in the house for ten minutes when she got to her feet and started for the bedroom she would be sharing. Her eyes beckoned DeeDee to follow.

Doug looked up quickly. "I was just going to suggest a quick game of Monopoly or Chinese checkers."

Her look was condescending, as though he could not be expected to appreciate her new sophistication – a sophistication which didn't accept such things as the games the Davis kids and Danny and Kay Orlis played together.

"Some other time, maybe," she said indifferently.

The tone of her voice made him cringe.

DeeDee couldn't help noticing, and she mentioned it as soon as they were alone. "I thought you liked Doug."

Sandy's expression was blank. "Doug? – Me?" One would think she had never even remotely considered bestowing her affection on one so young as her friend's brother.

"Last year during the basketball season he was all you could talk about." DeeDee was surprised at her own attitude. She was usually so angry with Doug and Del that she didn't know what to do, and she knew that Doug didn't like Sandy in the way she used to like him. But still, she didn't enjoy hearing Sandy talk about him.

"That was *last* year." She shrugged indifferently. "Now I find that I'm attracted to *older* men."

DeeDee's mouth sagged. "What?"

"Since I've been running around with Brenda, I've got to know some of the older guys, and I find that most of the boys my own age are so–so juvenile."

DeeDee jerked erect, her eyes blazing. "I don't think Doug is so juvenile."

That condescending smile came back once more.

"You think that because he's your brother. You have a prejudiced point of view." When she saw the anger and hurt mingling in DeeDee's eyes, she went on hurriedly. "Doug is a nice boy – a very nice boy. There's nothing wrong with him. It's just that some girls are more mature than others. And girls like that appeal to men who–who are more mature, like Steve Bell and the crowd he runs around with."

The conversation changed then, but as far as DeeDee was concerned, the evening had been ruined. She didn't know whether she was going to enjoy having Sandy stay with her or not. One thing was certain, Sandy was different than she had been when school let out last spring. DeeDee resented the change in her friend. She also resented her own feelings of emptiness and inadequacy. She resented the gulf that seemed to be widening between them. Brenda was taking her place in Sandy's life.

"It sounds as though she's a lot of fun." A wistful tone crept into DeeDee's voice.

"I don't think I've ever had a friend like her. She says what she wants to say and does what she wants to do. Nobody makes her do anything!"

DeeDee hesitated. She hadn't been invited to join Sandy and Brenda, but she had to ask. She had to be a part of their lives.

"I'd like to meet her sometime. I think I'd enjoy being with older kids too – those who aren't so juvenile."

Sandy frowned. "I don't think so, DeeDee. Frankly, you're not Brenda's type."

DeeDee was crushed. What remained of her weekend with Sandy had been destroyed beyond reclaiming. They went to bed at the usual time, and Sandy continued to talk about her new friend with growing excitement.

"What I like about being with Brenda and her friends is that nobody does anything he doesn't want to do. If I ask her what we're going to do, she always says that it doesn't make any difference. 'You do your thing,' she tells me, 'and we'll do ours.' "

"That sounds super!" DeeDee let her voice trail away. She didn't even know for sure if she was talking the way Sandy and Brenda talked. Oh, she had heard that kind of jargon around school, but there wasn't much of it that had rubbed off.

There was a long hesitation before her friend spoke again. "Whenever I get up-tight about Daddy and Mother being divorced, I can talk to Brenda and feel better."

* * *

Although Brenda kept looking for Sandy that morning to find out what her mother had said about going to Minneapolis with her, she was unable to find her. Sandy was waiting for DeeDee at her locker on the second floor.

"Hi, DeeDee!" she exclaimed as her friend came in with the others from the bus. "I've been looking all over for you."

DeeDee managed a thin smile.

A couple of girls were going by and Sandy lowered her voice. "Can we have lunch together? I've got to talk to you!"

DeeDee stared after her friend as she hurried away, curiosity gleaming in her eyes. She couldn't imagine what had happened that would cause Sandy to approach her the way she had. After all, she had hardly had anything to do with DeeDee since school had begun again.

And Sandy had been so mysterious about it. She acted as though the matter she wanted to talk to her about was terribly important. DeeDee couldn't remember Sandy's being that way since the awful days when her mother and dad had first talked about divorce.

Whatever it was, Sandy didn't want anyone else to know about it. She had stopped talking as soon as a couple of her old friends approached. She had done that before, but only when she wanted to tell DeeDee something that was terribly important.

Sandy had been running around with Brenda Ekberg most of the school year. She hadn't had time for DeeDee or any of the other kids in their grade. But now something serious had come up and who did Sandy go to? She didn't turn to Brenda. She turned to DeeDee!

It made her glow inwardly to think about it.

# CHAPTER 2

# PLANS AND DISCOURAGEMENT

DeeDee had to study for a test that morning, but it wasn't easy to keep her mind on American History. Her thoughts kept drifting back to Sandy and to the problem that seemed to be disturbing her so much. It had to have something to do with her parents. That was the only thing DeeDee could think of that would send Sandy running to her. Maybe her parents were thinking about getting back together and she wanted to ask DeeDee to have Danny and Kay pray about it. Or maybe she was finally seeing the kind of person Brenda really was and realizing that she shouldn't have anything more to do with her.

But somehow, she wasn't satisfied with either of these possibilities as the reason for Sandy's actions. Sandy was just being secretive. She wasn't as excited as she would have been if her parents had been talking about reestablishing their home. By the time noon came, DeeDee was so excited she almost ran out of her homeroom and down to the cafeteria, where Sandy was already waiting for her.

"Hi."

DeeDee's smile revealed her pleasure at having her friend ask to eat lunch with her again. It seemed like old times having Sandy wait for her in the cafeteria.

"Did you want to see me about something?" DeeDee spoke as guardedly as Sandy had earlier in the day.

Her friend nodded. "Let's get our food and go over in a corner where we can be alone. I've got something I've just got to talk to you about."

Numbly DeeDee followed her through the line. It was not until they were seated at a table in the corner, however, that Sandy began to talk. "I suppose you're wondering why I'm so mysterious about all of this." She spoke in tones little above a whisper.

DeeDee nodded.

"It's about Mother." Her lips curled around the word bitterly. "She found out that I was out at your place a few weeks ago, and she's been after me about it ever since. She doesn't even want me to talk to you."

"But why?" DeeDee's eyes widened. "I thought your mother liked me and Danny and Kay. You used to say that she *wanted* you to come out and see us. She thought it was good for you."

Sandy's mouth tightened. "That's what she used to say, but that was before Daddy started going to that church of yours. She doesn't want me to go out there because she's afraid I'll go to church with you and see him."

So that explained it! That was the reason Sandy hadn't been with her lately. That must be the reason she was running around with Brenda too. It was all her mother's doing.

DeeDee expelled her breath slowly. She felt better just knowing that it was something Sandy's mother had caused and not something she had done on her own.

Sandy waited for a moment or two, as though she was having trouble framing the proper words.

"I don't like to run the risk of getting you in trouble with Mother," she continued at last, "but I've thought and thought about it, and there's no other way."

"What do you mean?"

"I've got to come out to your place Saturday and Sunday."

"You know that you're always welcome at our place. Danny and Kay have said that dozens of times."

Sandy's expression did not change. "I've got to see Daddy."

DeeDee caught the tone of urgency in her friend's voice.

"It's terribly important! And if I don't come and stay with you, I won't be able to see him."

DeeDee's eyes narrowed. "Why couldn't you have Brenda bring you out to church?" she suggested. "You could see him that way." She didn't know why she had asked the question. The words had just slipped out.

Sandy seemed disturbed by her innocent query.

"I asked Brenda about it, but she said that the people at church would fall over dead if she came – and especially to *your* church."

DeeDee felt her temper flare briefly, but it subsided as quickly as it had surged.

"It will be all right if I come out and see you this weekend, won't it?" Sandy's voice was pleading.

DeeDee's flurry of anger disappeared. Sandy wanted to come and spend the weekend with her! She was actually choosing her over Brenda Ekberg! A smile split the seriousness of her features.

"Of course you can come. We'd love to have you."

Sandy sighed with just the proper amount of relief. "I knew I could count on you." She reached out and touched her arm. "I've been wanting to get out to your place for a long time, but Brenda and I have been doing so many things together that I haven't been able to tear myself away."

"Oh." DeeDee's newly found joy shriveled slightly. Maybe she wasn't going to replace Brenda in Sandy's affections after all.

Sandy saw the ice in DeeDee's manner and spoke quickly. "I didn't mean that the way it sounded. I enjoy being with you as much as I do with Brenda, but we've been so busy the last few weeks making all the groovy scenes she thinks of that we haven't had time for anything else." She paused, reflecting on the way she had used the words she had picked up from Brenda. They sounded so sophisticated and sharp when Brenda used them, but when she tried them herself, they rested uneasily on her tongue.

"I told her that I just had to come out to your place this weekend." Sandy lowered her voice once more. "It'll be all right, won't it?"

"Oh, sure." DeeDee couldn't help it. She was jealous of Brenda – jealous and more than a little curious about the secrecy of the projected visit. "But why don't you want anyone to know about it?"

"The two girls we saw in the hall this morning are the same ones who squealed on me the last time. And when Mother found out where I'd been, she talked with someone in the congregation. She found out that Daddy had been there that Sunday morning too, and she blew up!"

DeeDee hesitated. She knew what Danny and Kay would say if they knew that Sandy was coming to their house to visit without her mother's permission and against her wishes. As far as they were concerned, it wouldn't make any difference if Sandy did go to church with them or if her dad did enjoy seeing her when she came. They had some strong ideas about children honoring their parents, and they would expect Sandy to obey her mother.

The other girl noted the hesitation.

"It'll be all right, won't it?"

"I–I don't know what Danny and Kay would think."

Sandy jerked erect. "You mean they wouldn't want you to run around with me? Is that it? Am I such a terrible person all of a sudden that I'd contaminate you by coming out for a weekend?"

"Oh, no!" Concern quickly edged DeeDee's voice. "Oh, no! It's not that at all. It's just that they wouldn't like the idea of your coming out to see me if your mother didn't know and approve of it."

"They don't have to know, do they?"

DeeDee paused. She didn't like to think of deceiving Danny and Kay, but it was really such a little thing. And she couldn't do anything to drive Sandy away now – just when she had a chance to win back her friendship.

"I suppose not," she agreed reluctantly.

"Then it's all settled. I'll have Brenda bring me out about four-thirty Saturday afternoon. OK?"

DeeDee nodded. What else could she say? Sandy had always been able to get her to do almost anything she wanted her to do. It was especially important now when she had opportunity to be with her so little.

* * *

Thoughtfully Danny Orlis read the letter from Kent Gilbert, who was still at the school for the blind.

"He sounds terribly discouraged, doesn't he?" Kay said.

Danny nodded. He didn't know why, but for the last couple of years he had assumed that everything was all right with Kent and that he wouldn't have any more problems as far as his blindness was concerned. That made the letter all the more disturbing.

"Don't you think we should go and see him?" Kay asked. "Maybe there would be something we could do to cheer him up."

"I was thinking the same thing myself," Danny said, the frown lines deepening on his forehead, "but it will have to be next week. I've got to fly a couple of board members to the Canadian mission stations on an inspection trip. We won't be able to go over to the school until I get back."

"I'll write the superintendent and tell him that we'll be coming in a few days."

The next morning Danny left Fairview with the two board members shortly after dawn. When Kay finished her letter to the superintendent, the mail had come, bringing a letter from Mr. and Mrs. Gilbert. They expressed the same concern Danny and Kay felt. She read the letter over carefully a second and even a third time.

"We were quite disturbed when we saw him last week," Mrs. Gilbert had written. "Jill is with us now, you know, and he seems to miss her terribly. At least I feel that is the chief cause of his difficulty…. We've been praying a great deal about him and his problems."

Kay folded the letter carefully and returned it to

its envelope. Her own uneasiness grew. She wished she had talked with Danny about going on to the school ahead of time and spending a few days there visiting with Kent. She would have gone anyway, but she wasn't sure that was a good idea. She could still remember how the superintendent of the school had warned them about sympathizing with Kent. Going there and spending several days just could be the wrong thing, and she certainly didn't want to do anything that would make Kent's problem worse.

* * *

The day after Danny got back from the inspection tour, they flew up to the school for the blind to see Kent. They were half an hour from the airport when Danny radioed the manager and asked him to call the school and tell them when he and Kay would arrive. As they were taxiing up to the airport office, a new station wagon pulled in off the highway and stopped nearby. Kay squealed with delight.

"There's the superintendent, and he's got Kent with him!"

Danny brought the aircraft to a stop and shut off the engine. Kent had just got out of the station wagon and was standing with a hand on the door. He was trembling with excitement and expectancy.

"Kent!" Kay ran to him and swept him into her arms.

His lips quivered, and it was all he could do to keep from crying. "I–I sure am glad you came. I've been awful lonesome for you."

"You couldn't have kept us away."

Danny came up and took Kent's hand in his own strong fingers. "I'm sure glad to see you, Kent."

They rode back to the school in comparative silence. Danny and Kay hadn't been with Kent long when they realized that he was, indeed, defeated and miserable. He didn't have the smile he had worn the last time they had seen him, and when they walked across the campus, he didn't have the usual spring to his step. Kay went to the visitors' lounge with the blind boy, while Danny followed the superintendent into his office.

"I am glad you came to see Kent," he said, speaking quietly so his voice would not carry beyond the room. "Actually, he's having a bit of a problem again."

"So we've heard."

"It isn't anything of a serious nature. By that I mean that we've had no serious discipline problems with him like we've had with some of the other kids. It's more – well, I get the impression that Kent feels there's no use in his trying anymore."

Danny Orlis's frown darkened his bronzed young face. For a moment it looked as though he was about to speak, but instead he waited for the man across from him to continue.

"If there's anything a blind person has to have in

order to make a satisfactory adjustment and life for himself, it's an unquenchable spirit. Kent gave evidence of that for a while, but lately he's been acting defeated – as though he doesn't care whether he's ever going to be able to take care of himself or not."

Danny hoped he would have a chance to talk with Kent, but it seemed as if the boy sensed his purpose and was determined to keep him from it. When the time came for them to leave, Danny had the uneasy feeling that he and Kay had accomplished nothing. Once in the plane, he turned to Kay and asked her if she had had a chance to talk with Kent.

"A little." She was working her fingers nervously. "To tell you the truth, Danny, he acted as though he wanted to hide his feelings from us; but in spite of that they showed through. He's a terribly discouraged boy right now."

"That's for sure."

Kay breathed deeply. "We've got to be sure to remember him in prayer. His entire life could be ruined if he doesn't get hold of himself now."

# CHAPTER 3

# THE SCHEMER

Sandy was with Brenda on Friday night and was half hoping her friend would invite her to be with her on Saturday too. That was the reason she had suggested she go out to DeeDee's at four-thirty. That would give her and Brenda a fairly long afternoon together. Her friend had something else to do on Saturday, however, and came over to the apartment, where Sandy lived with her mother, shortly after four o'clock.

"I suppose you're ready to go out to the Orlis place now."

Sandy picked up her bag, thankful that her mother wasn't home yet. "I–I guess so."

They went out to the car together. Brenda was still so excited about the trip to Minneapolis that it was all she could talk about.

"I'm so glad you're going with me. It wouldn't be any fun to go alone."

"I'm glad too." She put her bag in the backseat and got in beside Brenda. It must be wonderful to have a car to use all the time!

"Our Minneapolis trip is going to be a real groove." Brenda's eyes were bright with anticipation. "When we get back, you won't be able to stand this dead place."

Sandy didn't know exactly what the older girl meant by that, but she didn't want to show her ignorance by asking. She glanced uneasily at Brenda. She was looking forward to the weekend in Minneapolis too – if things worked out so she could go. She always looked forward to being with Brenda. Excitement seemed to follow the older girl. But there were times when she found her companion's friendship somewhat frightening. It was almost as though she didn't know her or what she was really like. There was something mysterious about Brenda that both excited Sandy and repelled her. At times she had the uneasy feeling that she was beginning to walk a road she wasn't sure she wanted to be on.

"Where did you say we're going to stay when we get to Minneapolis?"

Brenda's laughter rang. "Tell me something, Sandy. Is this information for you, or is it something that you've got to tell your mother?"

Sandy Cole hesitated. Until that minute she hadn't realized there was any difference. This was one of the things that bothered her about her new friend. Brenda talked about lying to her mother as easily as she might talk about telling the truth. She made it sound as though it was the thing that all the smart kids did.

It wasn't that Sandy was always careful to tell her mother the truth all the time. She guessed that she had deceived her as often as most teenagers deceive their parents. But she had never been so open, so matter-of-fact about it.

Brenda must have sensed her surprise and concern.

"Don't get up-tight about it. Nobody tells their parents everything they do these days," she snickered. "Parents are so old-fashioned that they get shook up about everything."

Sandy nodded. She always agreed with Brenda about everything. The other girl expected it.

"Where will we be staying?" she asked again.

Brenda Ekberg lowered her voice slightly, as though even in the car someone might overhear.

"Well, you see, these friends of mine have this groovy pad on the second floor over a bar. I got another letter from them yesterday, and they said they're anxious to have me come. We can stay with them."

"Maybe they won't have room for me."

"Oh, they'll have room for you, all right. You're a friend of mine, so you'll be a friend of theirs."

"Are you sure?" The thought that she might not be welcome was devastating.

"You've got a hang-up that we've got to get rid of, Sandy," Brenda continued. "Of course I'm sure. If I weren't, I wouldn't take you."

Sandy sighed her relief. It was good to know that she would be as welcome as Brenda. That made her proud to have the older girl as a friend.

"Kids are always coming and going there. From what Sue writes, it's really cool. Nobody has to do anything he doesn't want to do. If you're sleepy, you can sleep. If you want to sit up all night and listen to records, you can do that. You just do your own thing, and nobody cares one way or the other."

Sandy's smile crept back to her lips. Her mother seldom made her do anything that she really didn't want to do, but there were times when she gave her a lot of static, and then she had to plead and storm and maybe cry a little to get her own way. It would be good to be someplace where she could do anything she wanted to do without any questions, even if it only lasted for a couple of days.

"That sounds like fun."

"Fun? It's going to be groovy just being able to do our thing without having someone burn us."

Sandy had only a vague idea of what Brenda was talking about. Actually, there were times when she wondered if Brenda really knew herself. She used those words as though she had memorized them and was sticking them into her conversation because that was the way her friends talked.

"I've been doing a lot of thinking about what you should tell your dad, Sandy. You've got to get him to let you go to Minneapolis with me. I don't know him, but he's probably like most dads – so square that he won't like the idea of your spending the weekend at a pad where there won't be any grown-ups to spy on you and make you do what you don't want to do."

Sandy knew that what Brenda was saying was true, especially now that her dad had become a Christian. One of the first things he would be sure to ask about would be the place where she and Brenda would stay in Minneapolis. He'd blow up for sure if he knew about Brenda's friends and the place where each person "did his thing" – whatever that meant. He wouldn't want her to go to a place like that. He'd act as though he didn't trust her.

Brenda continued. "You can tell him we're going to Minneapolis to do some shopping and that you're going to stay with me at my aunt's while we're there. He should approve of that, don't you think?"

Sandy nodded, but she wasn't really sure that he would approve of her going to Minneapolis with Brenda, no matter where they stayed. Lately he had had some peculiar ideas about what she should do and ought not to do. He treated her as though she were a baby.

Derision tainted Brenda's trilling laughter. "I've got

a great idea. Instead of that shopping bit, why don't you tell him I want to take a look at the university campus. That's something a lot of kids do. He won't suspect a thing."

Sandy thought about that momentarily. It could be that he would go for that idea. He had been talking a lot about wanting her to go on to school somewhere when she got out of high school. He might think this would be a way of getting her interested in it.

"He might think that's a–a groovy idea." Sandy used the word cautiously.

"And what he doesn't know won't hurt him a bit!"

They pulled into the Orlis yard and stopped. "Thanks." Sandy reached for the car door, ready to get out, but Brenda stopped her.

"I just thought of something. It might be a good idea not to say anything to DeeDee about what we're going to do or where we'll be staying. She might tell those religious weirdos she lives with, and they'd run right to your dad."

"Don't worry," Sandy assured her. "I won't tell DeeDee anything. You can count on it."

She got out of the car and took her overnight bag from the backseat.

"Don't forget. If you want your dad to give you the money to make the trip, you've got to con him. Tell him the things that he wants to hear."

Sandy walked slowly to the house. Going to Minneapolis sounded wonderful. Brenda was so exciting – so sophisticated for a high school junior. She could probably pass for 19 or 20 years old if she wanted to. And to think she chose to make Sandy her best friend! She could scarcely believe it was true. A girl like Brenda wanting to run around with her! It was–it was groovy!

But the big problem was going to be talking her dad into giving her the money she would need to make the trip. He wouldn't give in as easily as her mother would. He'd ask a lot more questions and demand a lot better answers. She had to admit it – Mother would believe anything she told her.

* * *

Danny and Kay Orlis were not expecting company other than Sandy Cole that weekend, but shortly after lunch on Friday, Mr. and Mrs. Gilbert called and asked if they could stop by to visit with them on the way home from seeing Kent at the school for the blind. The Gilberts hadn't planned to stay over-night, but they ended up doing so. They stayed up until midnight talking about the change that had come into their own lives and about Kent and Jill.

Jill, they said, was growing into quite a young lady. She was active in Sunday school and young people's at church and was a real leader at school.

"And when I think of the way we used to live," Mr. Gilbert put in, "and the change that has come over us and our two kids since they came to live with you, I can't thank God enough for sending them to your home."

Danny spoke up. "They've been a tremendous blessing to us too. It hasn't all been one-sided by any means."

"You have a special place in their lives too. We want you to know that. At times I think they love you and Kay as much as they love us."

At last Danny asked the question that had been weighing heavily on his mind since they had received the first letter regarding Kent. He had thought about it even more since they had been to the school for the blind to see him.

"How's he doing now? Is he still as blue and discouraged as he was a few weeks back?"

Mr. Gilbert's lips tightened thoughtfully. "I don't think he's quite as bad as he was. He seems to have times when he gets down and is more disturbed by his situation than he is at other times, but I believe he's getting along fairly well."

The boy's mother spoke up. "That's what we wanted to stop and talk with you about. It would be a real help to Kent if you could go over and see him again – soon. Maybe you could even have him over here for a weekend, if things worked out that way." Her cheeks colored. "I'm sorry. I shouldn't have asked you to invite him to stay with you. I know that you're very busy and that you have the triplets living with you now."

Kay answered. "Don't apologize. I think it's a wonderful idea, don't you, Danny?"

★ ★ ★

Sandy was so excited about her coming trip to Minneapolis and about having to talk with her dad about the trip that she had great difficulty in thinking of anything else. DeeDee and the boys wanted her to play Monopoly with them. She did for a while, but she scarcely knew whose turn it was, and she cared little about who was winning. She sat there, staring out the window and wishing that morning would soon come so she could talk to her dad about money for the trip.

He just had to let her have it. She'd simply *die* if he didn't.

DeeDee noticed that there was something wrong and asked her about it, but Sandy pretended to feel wonderful and professed not to know what her friend was talking about.

"Why, there's nothing wrong. I'm getting along fine. In fact, I'm doing great!" At that moment she wished she could tell DeeDee about the trip she and Brenda were going to be taking in a few weeks.

Hesitantly she weighed the matter. If DeeDee would promise not to say anything, maybe it would be all right to tell her. She wouldn't give Sandy's secret away. Sandy knew that. But she had given Brenda her word that she wouldn't tell DeeDee or anyone else. If she did tell her and Brenda found out, she would really be mad about it. She might not ask Sandy to go anywhere else with her, and that would be tragic. She didn't think she could stand to be without the friendship of Brenda Ekberg.

The following morning Mr. Cole was already at Sunday school when the girls arrived. Sandy's pretty young face lit up when she saw him.

"Oh, there's Daddy!" She rushed over to him, and he put his arm about her, squeezing her affectionately.

"I'm so glad to see you."

She pulled away from him slightly.

"Can we have dinner together, Daddy? There's something I want to talk to you about."

"Of course. I always enjoy having dinner with my best girl."

She was so anxious to talk to her dad about the trip to Minneapolis that she wanted to leave right after Sunday school, without staying for church. Her dad, however, insisted that they stay for both services, and she had to agree. She didn't want to risk making him mad now when she had something so important to talk to him about. As soon as church was over, she explained to Kay that she was going to have dinner with her father.

When the two of them were sitting across the

table from each other and had given their orders to the waitress, her dad wanted to know the reason for her need to see him. Hurriedly she told him about Brenda and wanting to go to Minneapolis with her for the weekend. At the mention of Brenda's name, he frowned.

"Is she the older girl that you've been running around with?" Disapproval edged his voice.

"And what's wrong with her?" she demanded irritably.

"I don't know that there's anything wrong with her, Sandy, but she doesn't appear to me to be the sort of girl that's good company for you." Sandy bristled. The conversation wasn't going the way she wanted it to go at all. Her temper flared. She might have known that he wouldn't want her to do anything at all that would be fun!

# CHAPTER 4

# FOILED

Sandy Cole pulled in a deep breath, fighting against the anger that flushed her cheeks and flamed in her eyes. When she spoke, her voice quavered with indignation.

"I thought you had always taught me to be fair with other people, Daddy," she countered. "You always said that I'm not to judge anyone else."

"You aren't judging Brenda when you compare what the Bible says about the way she should live with the way she really does live. She just doesn't measure up. It's the Word of God that's judged her."

She defended Brenda loyally. "The trouble is, you just don't know her the way I do. If you did, you wouldn't talk like that about her. I'm telling you the truth, Daddy. She is one of the nicest girls I know. I feel it's an–an honor for her to seek me out and want to be my friend."

Mr. Cole struggled to find the words to explain his position. It wasn't easy to try to reason with a girl Sandy's age, he had to admit. He found it much worse than trying to reason with her mother. "Brenda's older than you are, for one thing," he went on, "and she's probably permitted to do a lot of things you shouldn't be doing."

The flames in her eyes leaped high and her voice was taut with emotion. "You act as though I'm a baby, Daddy. I'm old enough to know what I want to do. I can look out for myself."

"Maybe so, but I don't think you should be going to Minneapolis or anywhere else with a girl like Brenda Ekberg. That's all there is to it."

Slowly the blood fled from her cheeks, leaving them sallow and lifeless. The corners of her mouth tightened.

"If you've already made up your mind that I shouldn't go, I don't suppose it would do any good for me to ask you to let me have the money I need to make the trip."

"That's right." He spoke reluctantly, as though he didn't like the idea of refusing her anything. He had so few opportunities to do things for her. Maybe he was just being old-fashioned, he reasoned. Maybe it wouldn't hurt anything for him to allow her to go to Minneapolis with Brenda. It was just for a weekend, and if they stayed at the girl's aunt's, everything should be all right. He was tempted to allow her to make the trip, but he knew he couldn't. It was wrong. He couldn't let her go to a big city like Minneapolis with another girl.

If it had been her mother who refused her, Sandy would have continued to beg. But she knew from past experience that it didn't do any good to try to coax her dad to do anything after he had made up his mind. He just wouldn't let her do anything that he had once told her she couldn't do. There was no pressuring him into anything.

"Well!" She drew herself erect indignantly.

She didn't know what was wrong with him all of a sudden. Why didn't he want her to do a little thing like go to Minneapolis for a weekend with Brenda? For the first time she was beginning to see why her mother got so angry with him! He could be the most pigheaded person in the world when he wanted to be. He was worse, even, than Danny Orlis, who wouldn't let DeeDee do anything that was any fun.

"Are you ready to leave, Daddy?" There was ice in her voice.

"Aren't you going to have some dessert?"

"No, thank you." She wrapped a cloak of silence about her.

* * *

Danny and Kay didn't have another opportunity to talk about Kent Gilbert and the problem he presented until after Mr. and Mrs. Gilbert had left. When they were gone Danny suggested that they do as the Gilberts had requested and ask Kent to come and spend a few days with them.

"Maybe having him in the house for a while again would give us the chance we need to help him."

"I want to have him come and stay with us for a while, Danny. You know that. But if they can't help him at the school, I'm not at all sure we can do anything."

"I'm not either, but we can try."

Her smile flashed. "It would be like old times to have Kent with us again, wouldn't it?"

Danny put his arm about her. "You miss the Gilbert kids, don't you?"

She turned to face him. "It isn't that I don't love the triplets. They mean everything in the world to me, but there are times when my heart aches to have Kent and Jill here again too."

Danny nodded. In a way, he shared Kay's feelings about the Gilbert kids. After all, they had lived in their home for more than two years, and they both had grown to love them. But he knew he didn't feel quite the way Kay did about them and that he never would. He supposed it had something to do with her being a woman. She had a mother's love for both Kent and Jill, the same as she had for the Davis triplets.

The next morning Danny phoned the school and asked the superintendent for permission to bring Kent home with him for a few days. The superintendent agreed quickly.

"In fact, I think it would be very good for Kent to spend some time with you in your home. It might help to shake him out of his despondency."

Danny wasn't sure when he would be able to get Kent. As usual, he had a lot of flying to do for the mission, but he promised to stop and get Kent the first time he was near the school for the blind.

* * *

Sandy Cole was furious with her father for refusing to let her have the money to go to Minneapolis with Brenda. For one thing, she didn't know what she was going to tell her older friend. That would probably be the end of their friendship for sure. Brenda wouldn't want to have anything more to do with her.

Without telling DeeDee about the trip, she talked the entire matter over with her. She had to have someone she could talk to. She got DeeDee to have lunch with her on Monday and told her part of the story.

"I never was so shocked and humiliated in my life." She was close to tears. "Daddy can be positively obnoxious when he is so unreasonable. He says that he doesn't even want me to be friends with Brenda! Can you imagine that?"

DeeDee sympathized with her.

"Parents do that, I guess. Danny makes some

pretty stiff rules sometimes too, and I can't always agree with them."

"When Daddy gets an idea into his head, he won't listen to anybody! He thinks Brenda is a bad influence on me, and nothing I can say will make him change his mind."

DeeDee did not reply, but she couldn't help feeling a quick throb of exhilaration. This meant that Sandy might have to quit running around with Brenda. At least she might not be with her so much of the time. And maybe – she could scarcely dare hope for it – but maybe Sandy would want to quit being with Brenda altogether and would start spending some time with her again.

But if Sandy had any plans for dropping Brenda, she didn't reveal them.

"If Daddy thinks I'm going to stop being friends with her, he's wrong. I'm old enough to make up my own mind about the people I want for my friends. I don't have to have anyone do that for me!"

That afternoon Brenda caught Sandy in the hall and wanted to know how she had made out talking with her dad.

"I thought maybe you'd give me a ring and tell me what happened, but you didn't." She spoke accusingly.

Sandy's cheeks colored. "I didn't have a chance."

That wasn't exactly true, but she had to lie to Brenda. She couldn't tell her the truth and let her know what a terrible person she had for a father.

"What did he say?" Brenda demanded. "Will he give you the money so you can go?"

"There are still a few details to work out," Sandy hedged.

The other girl frowned. "He didn't say that he wouldn't let you have the money for the trip, did he?"

Sandy retorted quickly – a little too quickly, she realized after she had spoken – but Brenda acted as though she hadn't noticed.

"Oh, no!" The second lie in as many minutes burned her lips. "Oh, no. It's nothing like that. It's just that–that–."

Brenda's laughter was reassuring. "You don't have to say anything else. I know how he talked to you. I used to get the same thing from my dad all the time. But we can't help it if they aren't with it. The trouble is that they just don't understand. Their minds are so bound up with making money and living their quaint little lives that they just can't imagine anyone wanting anything different. They just don't understand."

Sandy smiled gratefully. That was one of the nice things about having a wonderful friend like Brenda. She understood how it was with parents. She knew there were lots of times when a girl couldn't do everything she might want to do because of what her parents would say.

Brenda Ekberg continued, dismissing Sandy's father airily.

"I don't think you'll ever get your father to agree

to it, but what about your mother? What does she think about your going with me?"

"I–I–." Sandy swallowed hard. "I think everything is going to be all right, but I really don't know yet for sure. I still haven't talked to her about it."

"You'd better start talking." Brenda spoke with the knowledge of experience. "It may take you a little while to talk her into letting you go with me."

Sandy Cole promised Brenda that she would talk to her mother about making the trip to Minneapolis as soon as she got home that evening.

"And give me a buzz when you get her answer. You just have to go with me! It'll ruin everything if you don't."

When Sandy got home that night, she talked with her mother about spending the weekend in Minneapolis with Brenda.

"We just want to go so Brenda can look over the university," she said. "And, besides, we'll be staying with her aunt."

Surprisingly, Mrs. Cole frowned. "Why would Brenda want to be looking over a school so soon? She's only a junior, isn't she?"

Sandy's eyes clouded. "You know how hard it is to get into the school a person wants to get into, don't you? I think it just makes good sense to pick out a school early."

There was a taut silence.

"What about it, Mother? I can go, can't I?"

Mrs. Cole shook her head. "I don't see how we can manage it, Sandy, and besides, you're only 15."

"But Mother–." The girl's belligerence flared. "After all, I can take care of myself. I'm not a baby anymore."

"You don't seem all that big to me."

"Maybe not," she snorted, "but I am."

Mrs. Cole was still not impressed. "The thought of you two girls going to a city like Minneapolis alone, even for a weekend, frightens me, Sandy. I wouldn't be able to rest at all until you got back."

The girl snorted her indignation. "After all, we'd be staying with Brenda's aunt. There wouldn't be anything wrong with that, would there?"

Mrs. Cole shook her head.

"Maybe not, but I still don't like the idea. You can wait a few weeks until I can get off to go with you. We'll stay in one of the big hotels and do some shopping in the exclusive shops. That will be a lot more fun than going with Brenda."

"You sound just like Daddy!" Sandy exploded. She hadn't meant to mention her father. In fact, she had gone to great lengths to keep her mother from knowing that she had even seen him. But she had been so disturbed at her mother's attitude toward the Minneapolis weekend with Brenda that it had slipped out.

"Oh!" she exclaimed icily. "Have you seen your father lately?"

She nodded miserably. She didn't know why her

mother had to use that tone of voice when she mentioned Daddy. It was as though he was something awful – a convict – or something.

"I thought I told you that I didn't want you to see him anymore."

"But I–I–." Sandy squirmed miserably. "I wanted to talk to him about getting enough money to make the trip to Minneapolis with Brenda, so I went to see him. I knew it would be hard for you to give me so much at one time and–."

Mrs. Cole's eyes snapped. "And he wouldn't give it to you, would he?"

Sandy shook her head.

"That's just about like him!" Her mother's lips curled venomously about the words. "He doesn't care anything about you and me. When are you going to realize that, Sandy? He doesn't care whether you have a good time or not. All he can think about is himself and that precious church of his!"

# CHAPTER 5

# KENT'S VISIT

**S**andy was about to stomp out of the living room tearfully, convinced that her mother, too, had turned against her and was not going to let her go with Brenda. Then she paused and turned back, realizing the full import of what her mother had just said. She didn't know why she hadn't caught it before. But it was there, and she just might be able to use it to her advantage.

Her smile came slowly, and when she spoke, sarcasm tinged her voice. "Daddy said that he didn't care what you say, I still can't go to Minneapolis with Brenda."

If she had slapped her mother in the face, she wouldn't have got a sharper reaction. Mrs. Cole jerked erect, her eyes blazing. Twin spots of color deepened her cheeks.

"Oh, he did, did he? And exactly what business does he have trying to tell you what you can do and what you can't do? Doesn't he think I know what's best for you? Or what's he trying to do?"

Sandy shrugged. "He didn't say; he just tried to get me to promise that I wouldn't go. He said he was going to call you on the phone and tell you that I couldn't go with Brenda, but I told him that wouldn't do any good." She eyed her mother slyly. She had lied about what her dad had said, but this was an emergency – her only hope of getting to go. If this didn't work, there was no use trying anything else. She didn't know what she could do to get her mother to change her mind. And if she didn't get to go with Brenda to Minneapolis, her new friend would drop her, and that would be the end of everything!

"A lot of good it would do him to call me and tell me not to let you do something," Mrs. Cole snorted, her indignation building the more she thought about it. "It so happens that you're in my custody and I'm the one who has the right to say whether you do something or whether you don't. And for his information, I'm quite capable of deciding what's best for you and what isn't."

Hope began to flicker. Sandy realized that she used to play her parents one against the other to get what she wanted when she was in grade school and junior high. But she didn't know it would still work.

"Daddy didn't seem to think you're capable of telling me what I should do. He acted as though he was the one who should be telling me where I can go and where I can't."

Mrs. Cole was breathing heavily.

"That man!" She paced to the wall and raised her hand to straighten a picture that didn't need straightening. "If he interferes with the way I'm raising you, I'm going to take him to court. That's what I'm going to do! I'm not going to have him undermining my authority." Her voice choked. "Ever since we were married, he's treated me as though I don't know anything at all."

Sandy waited momentarily.

"What does that mean, Mother?" she asked. "Can I go with Brenda or not?" Her voice had just the right amount of doubt, as though she, too, felt that her mother wouldn't dare to let her do anything her dad said she couldn't.

"I haven't decided yet!" The words exploded from her lips. "But I can tell you one thing, Sandy. When I do decide, I'm going to make up my own mind. I'm not going to have to go to your father for advice."

Sandy thought about pressing the subject but decided against it. Instead, she went into her bedroom and sat down to study. She knew what was going to happen now. She had been over all of this before. She would wait for a day or two before talking with her mother again. She might even tell Mother that she wanted to know what to tell Daddy – that he was planning to get in touch with her to be sure her mother wasn't going to let her go to Minneapolis.

But she wanted to think about that for a time first.

She wasn't sure that she would have to go that far to get to do what she wanted to do. That was something she could save for another time.

Her mother hadn't yet told her that she could go, but she knew that she would. She could scarcely wait to tell Brenda how things were working out. She'd get a real charge out of it.

For a time that night, after she had gone to bed, Sandy's conscience bothered her. She didn't like lying to her mother, and she especially didn't like lying about her dad. It would only make things worse between him and Mother. But if they didn't want to be lied to, they should let her do things on her own once in awhile. They should realize that she was grown-up enough now to know what she wanted to do.

* * *

Danny Orlis had to fly to one of the southern states with one of the mission executives, so it was the end of the week before he was able to get over to the school for the blind to pick up Kent. The Gilbert boy seemed glad enough to see him when he got there. He wanted to know about Jim Morgan, Ron, Kay, and the triplets, but most of the time he was strangely quiet. He scarcely acted like himself. His face was somber and there was a petulant quiver to his lips.

"I stopped by to see if you would like to come back to Fairview with me and visit for a few days."

There was a short silence.

"*They* wouldn't let me go," he murmured, jerking his head.

"I talked with the superintendent, Kent. He thought it would be a good idea if you would go home with us for a few days."

The boy's voice brightened. "That would be swell. Only–." His manner seemed to change.

"Only what?"

"Only it won't be the same without Jill." He seemed apologetic that he missed his sister. "You know, she was always along on the other trips I made."

Danny knew what Kent was trying to say, and he felt sorry for him, but he couldn't let the boy know. If he did, he wouldn't be able to help him. "Well, DeeDee's there. You can tease her."

Kent grinned. "You know, it might be good to get out of this place for a little while. A guy can get soured on it if he has to stay here long enough."

Danny did not reply.

When they got back to Fairview the triplets were out at the airport with Kay to pick up Kent and Danny. The Davis boys hurried over to Kent, thrusting out their hands to take his.

"Boy, it's good to see you," Del told him.

"It's good to be here."

Then Doug broke in. "We're going to have a big time the next few days, and that's a promise."

For a few minutes, at least, Kent Gilbert seemed

to be carried along by their enthusiasm. Danny and Kay had written to him about Del's pets, and he asked about them all. He wanted to know if Jumper was still around and how Blackie was doing.

"Have you still got Blackie?"

"Del's still got him," Doug said. "And he still gets us into trouble every now and then."

Kent was thoughtful. "Can he really and truly talk?"

"We'll find him," Del promised, "and let you find that out for yourself."

As soon as they got home Del went out and called to his pet crow. It wasn't long until he brought Blackie inside with him, perched saucily on his wrist. Nobody had paid any attention to him for several days, so he was talking constantly.

"Have you got him?" Kent asked.

"Play ball!" Blackie screeched. "Run! Run, Doug, run!"

Kent's laughter trilled. "Does he always talk that much?"

"I think he must know we've got company and wants to do a little showing off."

"Boy, I'd give anything to have a pet like that. I just might have him in my suitcase when I go back to the school."

"If you do," Doug replied, "you'll probably have Del after you on the next bus. He thinks more of Blackie than he does of DeeDee and me."

The next morning when the Davis boys got up,

Kent was already sitting somberly in the living room. "Hi, Kent." Their voices were cheerful. "You sure get up early."

"I couldn't sleep." He was feeling sorry for himself again.

The boys ignored the tone of despondency that had crept into his voice. "Well, what do you want to do this morning?"

"It doesn't make any difference to me." He sounded as though there was nothing that they could think of that could possibly make him enjoy the day.

"There are a lot of things we can do, but Doug and I have been wondering if you'd like to ride over to Barney Aubichon's cabin with us to see him."

"Who's Barney Aubichon?"

As they sat at the breakfast table, Del told Kent about the elderly Indian and how he had helped him both to catch Blackie and to teach the bird to talk.

"Sounds as though he'd be an interesting guy to talk to."

"You can say that again! Barney's great."

When they had finished breakfast, the three of them went out to the barn and saddled their horses. Doug had Kent get in the saddle first. Then he swung up behind him.

"Think this horse'll ride double?" Kent wanted to know, concern coloring his voice.

"We'll soon find out."

"I hope we don't find out the hard way."

Doug started in the direction of the lake. "You don't have to worry about it. We ride this way a lot."

At that instant Blackie, who had been perching on the ridge of the barn, spied Del. "Play ball!" He swooped down and perched saucily on his master's head. "Blackie is a nice bird! Blackie is a nice bird! Three cheers for Blackie!"

In spite of his own dark mood that morning, Kent Gilbert laughed.

"What I wouldn't give to have that guy back at school with me for a little while. We'd have a wild time with him, I can tell you."

Blackie continued to chatter for a moment or two before flying off shouting, "Three cheers for Blackie!"

It was only a mile or so over to Barney's little cabin, but there was a stiff wind blowing out of the west. New snow bit their cheeks and drove the chill through their parkas into their very bones. Kent, who was not used to being outside a great deal in the wintertime, was shivering when they finally reached the cabin.

Barney was at home when they got there. He came out to the place where they were tying their horses, a broad grin lighting his dark face.

"Well now, I see you've got company this morning. I've been sort of expecting you."

They introduced him to Kent. The Indian man took the blind boy's hand and squeezed it warmly. "I've heard a lot about you from the boys, Kent. I'm sure glad you came to see me."

Kent liked the old Indian instinctively, but then, everybody did.

They went into the cabin, and Barney got out an extra chair so they could all sit down. Doug was the first to mention the trip Barney had been wanting to take that winter.

Barney shook his head. "I haven't got things worked out yet, but the Lord knows all about it. If He wants me to get back to Saskatchewan for a while to see my family, He'll work it out. And if He doesn't, then He doesn't want me to go home this winter, and that's fine too. Whatever He wants for me is best."

Abruptly he changed the subject.

Kent Gilbert couldn't help noticing how graciously Barney accepted the fact that he might not be able to do something it was obvious he wanted desperately to do. Kent pursed his lips thoughtfully. He wished he was more like the elderly Indian. Barney didn't waste any time feeling sorry for himself, that was sure. But he tried to tell himself that Barney wasn't carrying the kind of load he was carrying either. Now if he was–.

He stopped and took a deep breath. He had only known Barney for a few minutes, but he knew that even if the elderly man was blind, he would still be happy. There would still be laughter in his voice and a firmness to his step. In a way it made Kent ashamed of himself. Why couldn't he be more like Barney?

# CHAPTER 6

# THE PARTY

Sandy Cole waited with growing impatience for her mother to make up her mind about letting her go to Minneapolis with Brenda. In a way Sandy was sure she was going to get to go, and yet, until her mother actually told her she could, there was always the possibility that she would change her mind.

Brenda seemed even more excited about it than Sandy was. Two or three times during the next week she asked her about it.

"What does your mother say, Sandy? Has she told you whether or not you'll get to go?"

Sandy tried to sound more confident then she really was. "Oh, I'll get to go, all right. I don't have to worry about that. Mother isn't like Daddy. She usually lets me do anything I really want to do – especially if I coax long enough."

"That's the way my mom is." Brenda's tone was

derisive and mocking. "Of course, if she knew about some of the things I do, she might not be so anxious to let me do as I please. But, as she says, we're only young once. We should be able to have a little fun before we get married and settle down."

Mrs. Cole hesitated longer about letting Sandy know her decision than her daughter thought she would. Sandy was beginning to think she wasn't going to get to go after all. But in the end, her mother agreed.

"I don't feel quite right about letting you make a trip to a city like Minneapolis with only another girl to look after you, but I know I can trust you."

Excitement and relief gleamed in Sandy's eyes.

"Oh, Mother, thank you!" She kissed her impulsively. "Thanks loads!"

Mrs. Cole's face was grim. "And if that father of yours asks about it, you can tell him for me that I'm the one who makes the decisions about what you can do and what you can't do! And if he doesn't like it, he knows what he can do about it!"

Sandy could hardly wait to tell Brenda that she finally had permission to make the trip with her. Now she wouldn't have to worry about losing Brenda as a friend. Brenda would know that she was a person she could depend on.

* * *

Danny and Kay Orlis decided at the last minute to have a little party for Kent Gilbert while he was visiting them.

When Danny mentioned it to Kent, the boy wasn't even sure that he wanted to have a party. "I don't see how I could have any fun," he muttered. He didn't mention his eyes, but it was obvious that that was what he was talking about.

"We thought you would like to have some of your friends in to visit while you're home."

He shrugged indifferently. "I don't think I care to have much to do with the sort of guys I used to run around with. And I don't think they'd care to have anything to do with me either." He paused. "But maybe it would be nice to invite some of the kids in that Doug and Del and DeeDee know – if it'd be all right with them."

So it was decided that they would have a party after all. Sandy Cole was invited over Del and Doug's protests.

"This is supposed to be Kent's party," Doug said. "He's not going to want any girls there."

"But Sandy should come. She's my very best friend," DeeDee said loyally.

Kent decided the matter before it was referred to Danny and Kay. "I think it's OK for Sandy to come if DeeDee would like to have her. A party's not much of a party without some girls there."

Doug and Del both groaned audibly, but they knew when they were licked. They said no more about it.

Surprisingly enough, Brenda Ekberg asked Sandy if she could work it so she could get an invitation to the party too. Sandy stared at her. "You mean–you mean you actually want to go to a party at Danny and Kay's?" Sandy enjoyed going to see DeeDee. She was even looking forward to the party herself, but she couldn't imagine a sharp girl like Brenda asking for an invitation to the kind of party Danny and Kay would give.

"I think it would be groovy to go to one of their parties," Brenda said. "What do you suppose they'll do, play ring-around-the-rosy?"

Her tone made Sandy cringe inwardly. Brenda knew that DeeDee was a friend of hers. What would she think when she got to Danny and Kay's and found out what they were like? She wished she had courage enough to tell Brenda that she didn't think she should go to the party, but she couldn't refuse her request. Ever since they had started running around together, she had not been able to refuse Brenda's suggestions. Brenda had a way of getting her to do anything she wanted her to do.

DeeDee didn't like the idea of having Brenda come to the party either, but for a different reason. She had been thinking of the party as a means of getting Sandy back as her very best friend again. That was the reason she insisted on Sandy's being invited. Now Brenda would be there, and Sandy would be tagging along after her. But she couldn't think of a way to tell Sandy that Brenda wouldn't be welcome without sounding terribly selfish and spiteful.

"Sure you can bring Brenda. I'll tell Kay she's coming."

"Are you sure it'll be all right?" Sandy spoke as though she wanted DeeDee to say she shouldn't bring the other girl along. But she didn't.

"Of course it will be all right," DeeDee assured her. "Kay and Danny like to have our friends in. They won't care who comes."

She didn't tell Sandy that Danny and Kay had their home open to kids so they could have an opportunity to reach them for Christ or that they would never let her go anywhere with a girl like Brenda.

Sandy came over to the Orlis home the afternoon of the party and helped DeeDee and Kay get everything ready. It was going to be a nice party, she realized. If Brenda hadn't been coming she would have been looking forward to it as much as DeeDee and the boys were.

Mrs. Cole came to get Sandy in plenty of time for her to get cleaned up before supper. For some reason, known only to herself, she didn't object to Sandy's being with DeeDee or even being out at the Orlis home. The following week she might change her mind, but, for the moment at least, it was all right for Sandy to go there.

DeeDee offered to have Danny go into town to get Sandy, but she told her that Brenda was going to bring her to the party.

"She says she doesn't know anybody here, so she wants me to come with her."

As it was, Brenda and Sandy got to the party a little late. Brenda came in slowly, looking about, trying to gauge the reactions of the kids who were there. And Danny and Kay! She wanted to see the looks on their faces when they saw how short her skirt was. It was shorter than anything she had worn to school. Even her mother had protested when she saw her. But she wanted to startle Danny and Kay. They'd really get up-tight when they saw her.

She tossed her long hair defiantly. She didn't care what they thought, and she didn't care about their stupid party either. If they didn't like the length of her skirt, all they had to do was ask her to leave.

The kids in Minneapolis would get a charge out of that. She almost wished it would happen so she would have something to tell them.

But Danny came up to her and greeted her with a cordial grin, as though she was as square as that girl who lived at their place. Then he took her across the room and introduced her to Kent Gilbert.

"I've heard a lot about you, Kent." Her voice was warm and friendly.

"And where would you hear about me?" he asked. "My name hasn't been in the papers."

"You'd be surprised." Before he could answer, she took his arm. "Let's go over where we can be alone and talk."

Brenda guided the blind boy across the room to a corner where there were two chairs. They sat down side-by-side, but it was a moment or two before either of them spoke again.

"I'm curious about something, Kent," Brenda ventured at last. "Whatever made you come to a place like this for a visit?" Her lips curled about the words as though they were bitter.

"Because Danny and Kay and the triplets are just about the best friends I've got in the whole world, that's why." As he spoke, his voice firmed.

Brenda was surprised and a little disappointed by the fervor he showed. "And why have you got such a hang-up on them?" she wanted to know.

"If they hadn't taken my sister, Jill, and me into their home, I don't know what would have happened to us. We wouldn't be Christians now, that's for sure, and neither would our parents."

She stared at him incredulously. "Christian?" she echoed, her eyes widening. "What kind of bag is that?"

Kent couldn't remember when he had ever talked with anyone quite like Brenda. But she seemed to be so mixed up and so ignorant about what a Christian was. The kids over at the school knew more about God than she seemed to know.

"Did you know that Christ has a claim on your life?" He asked the question boldly, as though she should have heard that long ago.

She tossed her head defiantly. "You're putting me

on. Nobody has a claim on my life. I do exactly as I please! I'm my own boss."

Kent knew then why he was so interested in what Brenda was saying. She talked exactly the same way he had talked a few years earlier. She even sounded the way he must have sounded as he told everyone he was going to run his own life without interference from anyone.

"I used to feel the same way," he told her. "In fact, that's the reason I'm blind today."

Brenda seemed startled. "You're putting me on."

"I'm telling you the truth, Brenda. That's just the way it was."

"Exactly what do you mean by that?"

"I was determined to run my own life, and this is what happened." He touched one of his eyes with the tip of his finger.

She broke in caustically. "And what's the big hang-up about that? Everybody wants to run his own life, doesn't he?" she asked. "What does that have to do with your being blind?"

Kent went on slowly. "I had a bunch of buddies who were doing a lot of things they shouldn't have been doing, and I was right in with them all the time. What they didn't think of, I did." He went on to tell her how he had got into trouble with the law and had gone to a camp in Colorado where he had picked up the dynamite cap that later had cost him his sight.

She broke in rudely, her laughter harsh. "Oh, come off it! You're putting me on!"

"I'm giving it to you straight, Brenda."

She laughed again. "I'm not buying it, so you'll have to earn your brownie points somewhere else." She got to her feet and acted as though she was about to leave, but she sat down again impulsively. "Hey, I just thought of a groovy idea!"

"What's that?"

"What you should do is work things so you can go with Sandy and me to Minneapolis to the pad of a good friend of mine." She lowered her voice. "You'd get turned on with that crowd and forget this religious hang-up that's giving you so much trouble."

The corners of Kent's mouth tightened. "You mean you're going to take Sandy to a place like that?"

"What's the matter? Are you shocked?" Her voice was light and mocking.

# CHAPTER 7

# WARNING!

For a minute or two Kent Gilbert forgot about himself and his problems. All he could think about was Brenda and Sandy. He had never been to the sort of place Brenda was talking about, but he had heard plenty of the guys around the school talk about it. He knew what it would be like. Of course, he told himself, Brenda might only be putting him on, trying to get him shook up because he had talked with her about Christ and his own life. It could be that what she had said she and Sandy were going to do was a lie.

Yet he couldn't help being concerned about it. There was a possibility that she might have meant it. It was bad enough for her to go to a place like that, but to take Sandy with her was inexcusable! Just thinking about it made him furious.

Sandy seemed like a nice kid. Somehow, he had the idea that she was a lot like Jill, his own kid sister.

Sandy was a little harebrained and maybe stupid enough to let herself get involved with a girl like Brenda, but she surely wasn't Brenda's type. She probably didn't have the slightest clue as to what she was letting herself in for.

Brenda got to her feet, still taunting him. "I think I'll get my coat and go where the action is. This place is really a drag!"

Kent Gilbert scarcely realized she was leaving until he heard her heels click noisily on the floor as she hurried away from him. He got uncertainly to his feet, turning first in one direction and then another, as though he had suddenly lost his orientation. Kay saw him and came over to him.

"Is there something you want, Kent?" she asked.

He nodded. "Yeah, I was wondering about that girlfriend of DeeDee's. Has she been around tonight?"

"You mean Sandy?"

"Is she the one who came with that–that other girl?" he asked. "Brenda?"

"She's the one."

"Is she around here? I'd like to talk to her."

"I think so. She was here just a few minutes ago." Kay scanned the group quickly. Something in Kent's manner made it apparent that he had some strong reason for wanting to see Sandy, although he did not voice it. "I'll find her for you."

A moment or two later Sandy Cole approached Kent.

"Hi. Did you want to see me?" she asked.

"I sure did. I was afraid you had gone home already."

Sandy stood there, eyeing him quizzically. This seemed strange, having Kent want to talk to her. She had been with him once or twice when he was with DeeDee, but she really didn't know him well enough to have him want to talk to her. While she was still pondering the matter he spoke again.

"Let's go over and sit down where we can be alone. I'd like to talk to you for a minute."

She followed him, surprised at how well he was able to make his way through the room. It was almost as if he could see.

Kent spoke guardedly, listening for the footsteps of anyone who might be approaching. "I spent some time with your friend, Brenda, a few minutes ago," he told her.

Sandy's eyes gleamed. "Isn't she wonderful?"

He smiled slightly. "I suppose you could say that."

Anger glittered in Sandy's eyes. If Kent had brought her over here to criticize Brenda, she was going to walk off and leave him. That was one thing she didn't have to put up with.

"Didn't you like her?"

"Sure," he replied. "She's all right."

"She's the grooviest girl I've ever met." After Sandy had used the word, she wondered whether she had used it in the right way. She wasn't used to saying things the way Brenda did.

Kent did not say any more about the other girl.

"I brought you over here to tell you a story, Sandy," he began. Without waiting for her to say whether or not she wanted to hear it, he began to tell her about his own experiences when he was younger. He told her about having to come and live with Danny and Kay after the authorities took him and Jill from their own parents and how much he had resented the discipline they insisted on. He went on to outline the way he had got mixed up with a bunch of older guys and had wanted to do everything they were doing. He told her about the ring of auto accessory thieves and how close he had come to going to the reformatory for his part in their activities.

"If it hadn't been for Danny and Kay, I'd have ended up in the reformatory sooner or later. I was sure headed in that direction."

"Why are you telling me all of this?" she broke in sharply.

Kent acted as though he hadn't even heard what she had said. "You'd think I would have learned my lesson then, but I didn't. I went to a camp in Colorado and got into trouble with another guy at an abandoned gold mine. After I came home, I was fooling around with a dynamite cap I'd brought back with me from the mine. It exploded and cost me my sight."

She gasped. "How terrible!"

Kent continued quickly. "I'm no happier about being blind than you would be, or anybody else, but I've got to tell you that I'm glad it happened."

"What do you mean by that?"

"I became a Christian because of it, Sandy," he told her. "If I hadn't been blinded, I might have gone right on with my old friends, getting into more trouble and never realizing that I had to turn my life over to God."

Sandy Cole was horrified. Being blind, as far as she was concerned, would be one of the worst things in the whole world. If it happened to her, she didn't think she would be able to stand it.

"I don't see how you can even *think* that, let alone say it."

"That's because you don't know what it's like to let Jesus Christ have control of your heart and life. Now I'm going to heaven, and I'm not doing the terrible things that used to keep getting me into big trouble. I'd rather be a blind Christian than have my sight and be living the terrible kind of life I lived before."

Sandy breathed deeply, her emotions churning. She didn't know why she felt the way she did, but she was in agony.

"Why are you telling me all these things?" she insisted.

Kent was slow in answering, as though he didn't quite know what to say. "I don't have any right to butt in, Sandy, but when I talked with Brenda a little while ago, she told me that you've been running around with her."

Sandy stiffened. So that was it! Somebody else was going to try to tell her what she should do and what she shouldn't do. Wouldn't they ever learn that she was going to make up her own mind about her friends and that she was going to run her own life without interference from anyone else?

"So?" she said icily.

"I just hate to see a nice girl like you get mixed up with her, that's all."

"What do you know about her?"

"Enough to know that she's bad medicine for you, Sandy. She can get you into real trouble if you keep on running around with her. I'd hate to see that happen."

"You shouldn't believe everything you hear."

She got to her feet to leave, but Kent started speaking again, earnestly, as though he had to make her understand. "I haven't heard anything from anyone but Brenda, and that's the truth. But I know her type, Sandy. She's the same kind of person as the guys I used to run around with. And if you keep on being with her, it's going to make some terrible trouble for you. Believe me."

Sandy's anger flared. What difference did it make to Kent who she was with or what she did? Somebody must have asked him to talk to her. Danny or Kay probably asked him to get hold of her and try to convince her that she shouldn't associate with Brenda anymore. Well, it wasn't anybody's business what she did or didn't do. She was going to run her own life, and she didn't care who knew it!

"I'm sorry, Kent." Her lips twisted in derision. "But I really must be going!"

"Think about what I said," he urged her. "It's important, Sandy."

Sandy was almost sorry that she had agreed to spend the night with DeeDee after what had happened between her and Kent. He would probably try to corner her the next morning and preach at her again. But that wouldn't do him any good, she told herself firmly. She'd let him know what she thought of him if he tried that again. She wasn't going to let anyone come between her and Brenda.

In the bedroom after the party was over Sandy and DeeDee talked as they got ready for bed. DeeDee was still excited about the party. "Everyone seemed to have a nice time, didn't they?"

Sandy glared. "I suppose you could call it nice if you didn't care what you say."

Her friend looked up quickly. "Didn't you have fun?"

"I did until I got to talking with Kent Gilbert. That was enough to ruin the whole evening for me."

DeeDee's heart chilled. She had been so hopeful that Sandy would have a good time at the party. Now she acted as though she didn't want to have anything to do with DeeDee or anyone else in the family! She wished now that she had listened to Doug and Del and had not asked her friend to come.

"I thought you'd like Kent," she said numbly. "He seems nice to me."

Sandy snorted her indignation. "Wait until he starts telling you what to do!" She sat down on the chair near the bed. "You won't like it. Believe me!"

DeeDee caught her breath sharply. "What did he say?"

"He spent most of his time talking about Brenda and how bad an influence she is on me. If it had been anyone but Kent, I'd have just walked away from him. I don't have to stand and listen to people talk about *my* friends that way. I don't care who they are!"

DeeDee did not answer her. She felt the same way that Kent must feel about Brenda, but she knew what Sandy would think and say if she tried to tell her. She would never speak to her again.

Usually, the two girls talked for a long while before drifting off to sleep on the nights when they stayed together. But that particular night Sandy was quieter than DeeDee could remember ever having seen her. She didn't volunteer any comments, and she only answered DeeDee with a word or two. DeeDee was afraid that Sandy would blame her for the things Kent had said. That could only make matters worse.

Sandy's anger continued to build. She didn't know who he thought he was, trying to tell her what to do. And all that preaching! It was infuriating! He probably thought she would get the idea that he was some kind of saint, talking to her the way he did. Well, for all she cared, he could keep right on talking. He wasn't going to get any place with her! That was certain!

# CHAPTER 8

# SANDY'S DECISION

Lying there, staring up at the ceiling, Sandy thought of all the things she should have said to Kent Gilbert – the caustic remarks she could have made. She went over all the arguments that she should have given him – arguments he wouldn't have been able to answer.

But as the minutes dragged by, her fierce rage began to spend itself. After all, she did have to admit that it was just as he had said. He didn't have anything to gain one way or the other. He really didn't know whether he would ever see her again or not. The only possible reason he could have for talking to her the way he did must have been to try to help her.

And how had she treated him?

She cringed at the thought. She could still see his sightless face and the dark glasses that hid his expressionless eyes. She pictured the firm set to his jaw as he tried to convince her that she was going the wrong way on the wrong road.

DeeDee had told her part of the story about how Kent had lost his sight, but she hadn't realized until he had told her himself that *he* had actually been responsible for it. It wasn't just one of those terrible accidents that happen. It was caused by the way he had been living.

Probably what made her so angry was the fact that she had been so upset by the story he had told her. She was starting out exactly the same way he had gone. She was running around with Brenda, who was older than she was, and doing a lot of things no respectable girl would do. Sandy was already lying and deceiving her mother the way Kent had done with Danny and Kay. If she didn't get straightened out, she would soon be doing the other things Brenda did, and she didn't want that.

But as she lay there, it was not the story of Kent's life that affected her the most. It was another statement he had made – that he was glad he had lost his sight because going blind was the thing that had brought him to Christ.

She rolled over on her side and closed her eyes, trying to blot out the pleading look on his face. But closing her eyes did not help. She could still see him, as though he were standing in the room.

Being a Christian must be something wonderful if it could make a person be glad he was blind when his blindness had caused him to commit his life to Christ. Perhaps she was missing out on something after all – something that would give life more meaning than even the sort of life Brenda talked about all the time.

It was hours before she was able to go to sleep, and then she slept fitfully, waking every now and then. A great void seemed to grow within her being – an icy emptiness that took hold of her.

* * *

The next morning Kent, Doug, and Del were a little slower than usual in getting up. When they finally came to the kitchen for breakfast, Danny and Kay were sitting at the table. Danny looked up.

"Well now, I'm glad you characters finally got up. I was afraid I was going to have to go in and pull you out."

Del pulled out a chair and sat down, and the other boys did the same. "This is vacation, remember?"

Danny's lips parted, but before he could speak, Sandy Cole came into the kitchen. Her face was somber and looked as though she had been crying. They all spoke to her, but she did not reply.

Kay hurried over to her. "Sandy, is there something wrong?"

She started to speak but stopped and shook her head. Her eyes had already filled with tears. When she could finally force out the words, they were directed to Kent. "May–May I talk to you for a couple of minutes?"

He pushed back from the table, not believing his ears. "Me?"

She tried to swallow the lump that would not leave her throat. "I've got to talk to you!"

"Sure."

He went into the living room with her and sat down on the sofa. She found a chair across from him.

In the kitchen Doug and Del looked questioningly at Danny. "Now, what's this all about?" Doug asked.

Danny shook his head, warning them with his eyes to be quiet. Then he moved softly across the floor and closed the door so Sandy could feel free to talk with Kent without being overheard.

It was half a minute before either Kent or Sandy spoke. She coughed and ran nervous fingers across her young face.

"I suppose you're wondering what this is all about."

"As a matter of fact," he said, "I am."

Silence settled back over them – a heavy, oppressive silence that seemed to make it difficult even to breathe. Sandy squirmed uncomfortably, and for one frantic moment she began to think she had made a terrible mistake in talking to him that morning at all. She had to fight an almost overwhelming desire to flee.

"I–I–." She glanced about the room with

desperation. "I'm sorry I treated you the way I did last night. I shouldn't have said what I did. I know that you were only trying to help me."

"That's all right." One corner of his mouth tugged upward in a crooked smile. "I used to fly off the same way when anyone crossed me."

She touched her lips with the tip of her tongue. She was fighting with herself. Part of her wanted to break off the conversation while there was still time, but a stronger part of her cried out to Kent for help.

"I've been doing a lot of thinking about what you said last night." She paused and cleared her throat. "About how rebellious you were and–and how it caused your–." She was about to say "blindness," but for some reason that didn't seem kind enough. "How it caused your–your trouble."

Kent waited patiently. He didn't know why. It really wasn't in his makeup to be patient. That was one of the things that had been wrong with him lately. He had been impatient about being alone and having to stay at school when Jill was home with their parents, and that impatience had caused him a great deal of trouble. Now, however, it seemed that he should wait until the girl across from him was able to continue talking.

"I couldn't sleep last night because I kept thinking about the things you told me. I don't want to get into the same kind of trouble you got into – or worse. I want to be a–a good person."

Kent nodded. "Most of us do. But we want to have our fun too, and Satan tries to persuade us that we can't have any fun unless we do things his way. That's just one of the big lies he tries to make us believe. Christians can have a lot more fun than anyone else, and it's clean fun that isn't going to mess up anyone's life."

There was a long hesitation. In one way Sandy seemed to indicate that the conversation was over. He heard her stand once and take a step uncertainly. But she came back and sat down again, as though there was something else on her mind – something more important than what they had already talked about.

He took a deep breath. It wasn't easy for him to talk to her about her need to turn her life over to God, but he had to. There was no way to avoid it!

"If you want to be sure you're not going to mess up your life, Sandy, you need the same thing I have."

"You mean – religion?" She had difficulty in saying the word.

"No, I don't mean religion. Lots of people have religion. What you need is the Lord Jesus Christ. You need to accept Him as your Savior. Then you can depend on Him for the help and strength you need to live the way you should."

He was surprised at how easy it was to talk to her about her need for Christ after he got started. He couldn't remember all the Bible verses he wanted to quote to her, but he did know his own story. He told her how upset he had been when the doctor in Minneapolis had told him he would never see again. He had already gone over that with her the night before, but now he had an added purpose.

He told her how the pastor had come to Minneapolis and talked with him, showing him that life hadn't ended for him. He had told him that with Christ he could have a full, rich, satisfying life – regardless of the circumstances in which he lived.

"And I've found that's true," he added. "Oh, I get down in the dumps once in a while, but that's my fault. It isn't God's." As Kent talked about that, he realized the full import of what he was saying. God hadn't promised him, or anyone else, an easy, soft life as a reward for following Him. He promised strength and help to rise above whatever conditions he found himself in and to be happy whether he was blind or not. All he had to do was ask God for it and believe He would provide, and he would have a victorious, happy Christian life. "You can have a life like that, Sandy. I can have it, and so can Brenda and your mother and anyone else. Instead of religion, you need a new life–life in Jesus Christ."

Sandy brushed her hair back from her eyes. For a brief flutter of time, she thought of Brenda. Her sophisticated friend would laugh scornfully if she ever decided she wanted to give her life to God the way Kent said she should. But at that moment, what

Brenda would say made no difference to her. "I'd like to have that new life."

Kent and Sandy knelt in the living room. She wasn't able to pray at first. She didn't know how. But with his guidance she stammered through a short little prayer, telling God she was disgusted with the kind of life she was living and asking Him to forgive her sin and make her a child of His.

As Sandy Cole prayed, a new exultation and sense of accomplishment surged through Kent Gilbert. It wasn't pride in the fact that he had been the instrument God had used to bring Sandy to Himself. It was more than that – it was a feeling of joy that he, of all people, was able to serve. For the first time he was made to understand that just because he couldn't see, he didn't have to sit on the sidelines and expect to have other people do the work. He could be a useful member of society. There were things he could accomplish. He was far happier at that moment than Sandy could ever be – or so it seemed to him.

# CHAPTER 9

# A CHANGE IN PLANS

Sandy and Kent went back into the kitchen then and Sandy told Danny, Kay, and the triplets what had happened. DeeDee cried. She couldn't help it. And so did Kay. That was a bit bewildering to Sandy. She couldn't understand why they should be so happy about something that had happened to her that they would cry, but she didn't say anything. She felt like crying too, especially when Danny suggested that they all pray for her. Each of them asked God to help her live the kind of Christian life that would make other people want to be Christians too.

Mrs. Cole had given Sandy permission to spend the weekend at the Orlis home, but after what had happened, Sandy felt she had to go back to the apartment she shared with her mother. On the way back to town she was quieter than usual. Kay had explained how important it was for her to let people know that she was now a new person in Christ. While Kay was talking, she had agreed, thinking it would be easy to talk about this new faith of hers – as easy as it was for DeeDee and the boys and Danny and Kay. Now, however, her throat constricted, and perspiration pearled her forehead at the very thought of telling her mother and Brenda. They were the ones who bothered her the most. They were the ones she had to tell first. She realized that instinctively.

Sandy glanced at her watch. Her mother probably wouldn't be home. She had said something about going to a neighboring town for lunch and to shop with some of her friends. That would let her talk to Brenda first.

In a way it was going to be much harder talking with her friend, but in another way, she was glad she could do it without having to wait. It was almost as though she was afraid she might change her mind and go to Minneapolis for the weekend in spite of the fact that she was now a Christian.

She thanked Kay and DeeDee once more and got out of the car.

"We'll be praying for you," Kay called after her.

She didn't look back, but Kay's words were a comfort to her – a little measure of assurance that she might be able to get through what she knew she had to face.

As she suspected, her mother was gone. There was a note for her on the kitchen table in case she did come home. It said there was something to eat in the refrigerator and for her to be sure and do her dishes.

Sandy laid the note back on the table and went to the telephone to call Brenda.

"Oh, Sandy, I'm so glad you called." Brenda's voice trilled. "What happened out there after I left?"

"Nothing much." Sandy had trouble getting the words past her lips.

"Did they try to convert you?" Derision honed a fine edge on her voice.

Sandy paused so long that Brenda feared she had hung up. "Sandy, are you there?"

"Oh–oh, yes. I'm still here."

"I don't blame you for being shocked. I was, too, when that Gilbert character tried to snow me with that religion bit of his. But I fixed him. I asked him to go along to Minneapolis with us so we could help him get rid of his hang-ups."

"I felt sorry for him, being blind and everything, but he's really weird. As far as I'm concerned, he can do his own thing, even if it is that oddball religion of his. But it's not my bag, and I don't want him trying to shove it off on me."

Everything Brenda was saying made it harder for Sandy to talk to her, but there was no other way. She had to go through with it.

"Mother's gone for the rest of the day, Brenda. Could you come over for a little while?"

The older girl caught the strange, taut tone in her

voice. "You sound up-tight, Sandy. What's wrong? Did your mother change her mind?"

"No." She spoke quickly. "No, she hasn't changed her mind as far as I know."

Brenda sighed her relief. "Good. I'd just die if something happened to spoil our trip."

Sandy did not reply, but her friend was too excited to notice. "I'll be over in 20 minutes, OK?"

Sandy watched uneasily for Brenda to come. In her mind she had worked out exactly what she was going to tell her older friend. It might just shake her too. And – she could scarcely dare to hope for anything like that – but maybe Brenda would make a decision for Christ too.

The excitement and optimism Sandy had known earlier in the day when she first made her decision for Christ came rushing back. Brenda was sharp enough to see that the sort of life she was living would only lead to trouble. Surely she wouldn't want to keep on, when only disappointment and heartache would come of it. She would become a Christian, and the two of them could talk to the rest of the kids they knew at school. Maybe all the kids in their crowd would become Christians.

She was still thinking how wonderful that would be when a car stopped out front and she heard the door slam. She went quickly to the window and looked out. There was Brenda walking toward the apartment house.

A chill swept over Sandy. How could she talk with someone like Brenda about the Lord Jesus? How could she even tell her what had happened to her when she already knew what Brenda would say? Two days after vacation was over all the kids in school would be laughing at her.

Sandy knew that her cheeks were ashen when she went to answer the door. Brenda came in, tossing her long hair to get it out of her eyes. "Hi."

Sandy answered weakly.

"What are you so up-tight about?" Brenda went over to the divan and plopped herself down.

Sandy sat across from her, determination fixing her mouth sternly. "I–I just wanted to talk to you." The other girl pulled herself erect. "OK, let's hear it. What's your hang-up?"

Sandy cleared her throat and disengaged her hands from each other long enough to wipe her face with trembling fingers. After this afternoon, Brenda would probably never speak to her again.

By this time, the other girl realized that Sandy was seriously disturbed about something.

"You really are hung up, aren't you? Tell Mama Brenda all about it. She'll kiss it where it hurts and make it well."

"I–I–." Sandy's gaze met Brenda's miserably. The words refused to come.

Brenda opened her purse, took out a cigarette deliberately, and lit it. She knew Sandy didn't like to have her smoke in the apartment, even though her mother smoked. They used different brands, and she had been afraid her mother would find out Brenda smoked and would want her to quit running around with her for that reason. Usually Brenda was careful about it, but this time she pulled an ashtray over and filled her lungs with warm smoke.

"You don't need to get up-tight about a little cigarette. This one's tobacco – not grass."

"I knew it wasn't marijuana." She didn't know why it was that she was always so defensive when she was with Brenda. It was as though she had to apologize for any standards she had.

"I know you wouldn't be stupid enough to fool with marijuana," she continued.

Brenda laughed. "You've got a lot to learn, Kid, a lot to learn."

"Have you?" Sandy didn't know why she had asked that question. It was probably because she was so shocked by the implication of what her friend had said.

"That would be telling." Slowly the taunting smile left her petulant young face. "You didn't call me up and have me come over here to tell you that I might be smoking a stick of pot once in a while to turn me on. What's the pitch, Sandy? What's got you so hung up?"

Sandy got to her feet with some deliberation. "You're not going to like this, but–."

"Oh?" Her friend broke in rudely, anger flecking

her eyes. "As a matter of fact, I don't like it already. You call me over here and don't tell me what the big scene's all about. Come on, let's have it."

"I've got something to tell you, Brenda." She was so disturbed that her voice was unnaturally harsh. "I can't go to Minneapolis with you."

Brenda Ekberg stared at her as though she could not quite believe what Sandy was saying. "I thought your mother said you could go. What gives?"

"She did say I could go, but I–."

"You're putting me on!"

Desperation glinted in Sandy's eyes. How could she tell Brenda Ekberg that she didn't want to go to Minneapolis with her now? How could she explain to a person like Brenda that she was letting God have complete control of her life now?

Brenda drew herself up indignantly.

"The least you can do is give me an explanation." She was so angry that she forgot to use her new vocabulary. "You realize that I've gone to a lot of trouble to get this lined up for you. The kids are going to think you've really copped out."

"I'm sorry, Brenda."

Brenda's manner changed. Anger gave way to a kind of desperate pleading. "I've tried and tried to get other kids to go with me, but none of them can. I've been counting on you. I won't have anyone to go with if you don't go." She brushed her hair from her eyes with a nervous gesture and leaned forward. "You'll have a great time."

Sandy did not answer her immediately, so she went on. "I'm going to make a confession to you. I've never been to this pad – this apartment – either. And I've never spent a weekend with these kids. But they've told me how groovy it is, and I finally agreed to go." She reached in her purse and took out a letter. "Here, I'll let you read what they wrote about your coming with me. They're as excited about it as I am."

But Sandy did not take the envelope.

"I'm sorry about that too. It looks as though I've made a real mess of things for everybody, but I still can't go!" The words slammed out so harshly that Brenda flinched.

While Sandy was trying to put the words together to tell Brenda what had happened to her, her friend stood tauntingly. "I know what happened to you. That blind religious nut got to talking to you, didn't he? He zapped you with religion!"

"I did talk to Kent." It was strange how she had lied to her mother and dad so quickly only a few days before, but now the thought hadn't occurred to her.

"I should have known. And he told you that I'm not fit company for you, didn't he? He thinks I'll contaminate you or something."

A sudden earnestness crept over Sandy. "Don't you see? He's blind today because he was so determined to have his own way and do everything he wanted to do."

Brenda lit another cigarette and blew a thin plume of smoke in Sandy's direction contemptuously.

"He's blind, all right. And not only in the way you're talking about."

The silence was a cloak about them. Sandy found it hard to continue, but there was no turning back – no stopping what she had to say. "I can't let Kent take all the blame for my not going with you. There's another reason."

"Like what?" She sat on the arm of the chair.

"I committed my life to Christ this morning. That's the real reason I can't go with you to Minneapolis."

Brenda stared, incredulity marring her face. "What did you say?"

"Oh, Brenda! It's the most wonderful thing that has ever happened to me. I met the Lord Jesus Christ and He's changed me. I'm not the same Sandy Cole that you knew."

"So that's it! Zapped by religion!"

"It isn't religion." All of Sandy's fears about talking to Brenda were gone. The only thing she cared about now was finding the words to explain to her friend the wonderful change that had come into her life. "It's like Kent says – lots of people have religion. There are people here in America who worship money and the things it can buy, and they have religion.

Being a Christian is an experience – a whole new way of life–."

Brenda broke in, venom poisoning the tone in her voice. "So that's it! He did get to you, and you fell for it! You bought the whole religion bit!"

Her laughter rang. Sandy Cole was watching with growing surprise, as though scales had suddenly been removed from her eyes so she could see Brenda as she really was. What she was seeing was a coarse, petulant girl who could be attractive if she fixed her hair, cleaned up and wore some decent clothes. She couldn't see how she had ever been drawn to Brenda or why she had enjoyed her company.

"I'm glad I found out what you're really like!" Brenda was so loud in her anger now that she could be heard in the next apartment. "When you get tired of this religious kick, you'll come crawling back, wanting to run around with me again. But now that I've found out what a square you are, I wouldn't take you anywhere, even if you begged me to!"

She buttoned her coat, whirled, and stalked out of the apartment. She didn't even bother to close the door behind her.

Sandy watched until Brenda screeched out of sight in her car. Then she went over and closed the door. She was still breathing heavily from the strain of facing up to Brenda and withstanding her friend's scorn. It hadn't been easy for her to keep from matching temper for temper during their conversation. To be completely honest with herself, she had to admit that she had been angry, but she had been able to control her voice, at least enough so that Brenda hadn't been aware of the way her spiteful voice had ignited Sandy's own heart. She was thankful for that.

She went over to the sofa and sat down, wondering whether the time would ever come when she would be able to control her temper when another person talked to her the way Brenda had. Kent spoke about victory and living a Christian life. She wasn't sure just what he had meant, but she had a good idea that it didn't mean getting mad the way she had just now. Sandy sighed deeply. She had so much to learn about this business of being a Christian. She hoped God wouldn't get tired of forgiving her.

Suddenly Sandy had an overwhelming desire to call DeeDee and tell her what had happened. And she had to see her dad and tell him what had taken place in her life too. She knew how happy he would be to know that she was a Christian, the same as he was. She wondered if he had been praying for her. Maybe DeeDee, Del, and Doug, and even Danny and Kay had been praying for her too. Maybe that was the reason she had listened to Kent when he had talked to her. She wanted to remember to ask DeeDee about that.

There were so many things she was going to have to ask DeeDee about. She had heard the minister read from the Bible the few times she had gone to church with her Christian friend, but she didn't know much about what was in it. She wouldn't even have known that a Christian should read the Bible if Danny and Kay hadn't done so when she was visiting in their home. Maybe her dad would buy her a Bible if she asked him to.

Then there was her mother. That uneasy feeling came back. It was going to be almost as hard for her to talk with her as it had been to talk to Brenda. There were some things she had to get straightened out with her, and that wasn't going to be easy. She had been lying to her mother for the last few weeks and deceiving her in other ways. She would have to tell her about that and ask her forgiveness.

Come to think of it, she would have to do the same with her dad, but it wouldn't be hard to talk to him. He was a Christian himself. He would understand.

She waited up for her mother until almost midnight, but finally she got so sleepy she had to go to bed. When she got up the next morning in time for Sunday school, her mother was still in bed. Sandy went in to wake her up, but she protested sleepily.

"Go away and let me sleep. This is the only time I can stay in bed." An accusing tone crept into her sleep-slurred voice. "You know that, Sandy. You know better than to wake me up on Sunday morning."

"I–I'm sorry, but there's something I've got to tell you."

"Can't it keep?"

Sandy's temper flared. She was about to retort hotly when she remembered what Kent had said. She was glad that he had told her it wouldn't be easy to live a Christian life. If he hadn't, she would have thought there was something wrong with her or that she wasn't even a Christian.

# CHAPTER 10

# THE INTERVIEW

At the Orlis home, Kent Gilbert was much happier than he had been since those dreadful days following the accident that had blinded him. At the breakfast table he felt he had to let the whole family know how much coming to stay with them had done for him.

"When I came, I was feeling so sorry for myself I could hardly stand it. It was almost as bad as it was before I became a Christian. I had almost reached the place where I was beginning to think God must not know or care that I'm blind and need His help. I felt there wasn't anything that I would be able to do – that I would have to depend on others to take care of me the rest of my life."

He grinned suddenly. "And then I had a chance to talk to Brenda Ekberg about what happened to me. It didn't do any good, but I got to talk to her anyway. And then there was Sandy. I don't think I've ever had anything so wonderful happen to me since I gave my heart to Christ right after the accident." He paused. "It makes a guy feel as though he is good for something after all."

* * *

Sandy Cole left home early Sunday morning, before her mother got up, so she could have time to talk with her dad before Sunday school. When she told him the good news, he was thrilled. "You'll never know how happy that makes me!"

She told her father how sorry she was that she had lied to him about the purpose of the trip to Minneapolis. Mr. Cole reminded her that as a Christian she would now be able to depend on the Lord to help her do and say what was right.

When Sandy got back to the apartment after church, her mother was gone. A note on the kitchen table said she would not be back until late that night.

She didn't get to see her on Sunday night, and the next morning her mother was scurrying about so much, trying to get to work on time, that there was no opportunity to talk with her then. It wasn't until Tuesday, when Mrs. Cole got off work, that Sandy could spend some time with her.

By this time, the girl had thought and rethought everything she was going to say. But, as she feared, when she tried to tell her mother about her decision for Christ, it came out all wrong.

Mrs. Cole sat stiffly on the kitchen chair across the table, nervous fingers working a tea towel into a tight little knot. The color faded from her cheeks, and her mouth straightened into a thin band of steel.

"Is this one of your father's little games?" Contempt marred the usual softness of her voice.

Sandy looked at her in growing desperation. "Daddy didn't have anything to do with it, Mother."

Mrs. Cole straightened. "Don't try to tell me that. I'm not completely naive."

Tears came to Sandy's eyes, but her mother continued talking. "I suppose the next thing you'll tell me is that *I* should get this religion of yours. Then I won't be able to resist your father's pleas to take him back. Well, it's not going to work! So you'd just as well forget trying to get me to go back to him. I'm through!"

Sandy ran out of the room. She had thought things would be better once she decided to follow Christ, but they weren't. They were worse – much worse.

First Brenda had turned on her, and now it was her mother. For a brief instant she wondered whether it was worth it. She wanted her mother and dad to go back together more than anything else in the world. That was all she had thought about for months. And, since she had become a Christian, it was the most important thing in the whole world to pray about as far as she was concerned. She went into her bedroom, closed the door, and dropped to her knees.

* * *

Brenda didn't know why she was so upset by the things Sandy had said to her, but she was. Sandy seemed so happy and so excited about this new way of life she had discovered. When she talked about being a follower of Jesus Christ her entire being seemed to glow. Brenda knew she had ridiculed her, but deep within her she longed to have the same peace and the same radiance.

At first she was about to call Sandy back and talk with her, but she just couldn't. That would ruin all the fun she had planned. Still uneasy, she tried to find something else to do.

However, the day before going to Minneapolis for the weekend, she contrived to meet Sandy on the street to see if she would change her mind.

"It's not too late, you know."

"But it is. It's much too late."

"You're just stoned on religion right now, that's all. You've freaked out. When you come down, you'll see how square you've been."

But Sandy was firm. "I know what I have now, and it means more to me than anything else in the whole world."

"You sound just like that Kent Gilbert." Her laughter was harsh and taunting.

Sandy remained motionless. There were so many things she wanted to say to her friend, but the words choked in her throat. It was as though she couldn't bring herself to say them. Brenda realized it was useless to plead further.

"While I'm gone, why don't you pray for me?" she mocked.

* * *

Sandy Cole didn't see Brenda for several days after the girl got back from her weekend trip. When she did talk to her, Brenda's eyes were still bright and hard with excitement.

"You should have been with me. It was groovy!" She seemed to be trying hard to make Sandy realize how much fun she'd missed. "But you must not have been praying for me because I had a great time."

Sandy thought Brenda was through with her – that she would have nothing to do with her anymore – but that was not the case. Brenda phoned her on several occasions, and at least twice she stopped to see her.

"Just thought I'd check to see how that religion of yours is wearing."

"I'm happier than I've ever been."

Brenda seemed surprised. "You mean you haven't found out yet that it's not your bag?" For an instant the derision was gone from her voice. "Haven't you got tired of going to church and praying and all that junk?"

"No, and I'm sure that's not going to happen, Brenda."

"Don't bet on it."

* * *

Coach Alex Smith was enjoying the vacation from classes at school. He was through with football, which was his major responsibility, and there was little he did with the basketball team. He was out every night for practice, but the head coach had the major load. For that reason, the midwinter holidays were actually a short vacation for him. He helped his wife, Robin, around the house, they entertained frequently, and they slept late in the mornings. It was one of the most enjoyable periods for him since they had moved back to Fairview.

"You know, Robin, I love to coach, but I am beginning to think there's something else in the field of teaching that interests me more than coaching, and that's counseling."

Her gaze met his.

"Oh, don't get me wrong. I don't plan on giving up football. But I was just sitting here thinking about the chances I've had to talk with kids who are all mixed up. It's a real challenge."

Robin nodded.

"These kids have some terrific problems, and if they're going to get them straightened out without torpedoing their lives, they've got to have someone to talk to – someone who understands them and wants to help them."

For a time Robin sat there thinking about what he had said. It was true that Alex did know a lot about people and what made them do what they did. And everyone liked him, especially the school kids. She could tell that by the way they spoke to him on the street. He should be able to help a lot of them.

* * *

Toward the end of the week, Alex took the car to the service station where he had first worked after quitting high school following their marriage. He was going to have it serviced and have the tires rotated. He told Robin he would probably be gone most of the morning.

She was working around the house when there was a knock at the door. Mildly disturbed, she went to answer it. It was probably some salesperson. She didn't know why people had to bother her in the morning when she was trying to get her work done.

She was surprised when she opened the door and saw a slender, long-haired girl standing there.

"Hello. I–I'm Brenda Ekberg."

"Oh, yes. I've heard my husband mention you. Won't you come in?"

Uneasily, Brenda took half a step inside, but not far enough so Robin could close the door.

"Is Mr. Smith home?"

"He isn't here right now. Is there anything I can do for you?"

Brenda looked about uncertainly as though, now that she had come, she was wondering why she was there. There was no color in her cheeks, and her shoulders twitched nervously.

"Oh, no!" The words exploded from her lips. "Oh, no! I just wanted to see Mr. Smith, but I can see him some other time."

"I can call him and ask him to come home."

"Don't do that!" Brenda panicked and Robin half expected her to bolt down the steps. "I–I just had something I wanted to talk to him about. I can see him later."

She moved backward half a pace. Her eyes were wide with terror, like an animal about to flee.

"Why don't you come in and have a cup of hot chocolate with me?" She touched the girl's elbow as though to usher her into the kitchen. "Before we've finished, I'm sure he'll be here."

Brenda jerked away.

"I can see him sometime next week, or even after school starts again." Tears were glistening in her eyes. "I–I'll get in touch with him later."

Robin made no further effort to keep Brenda there until Alex could talk with her. It would have been useless. Instead, she stood at the window and watched while the girl got into her car and drove away.

Still troubled by the unexpected visitor, Robin went about her work. When Alex came home, he was surprised to hear that Brenda had come to see him.

"She's one person I've been afraid I could never get through to at all. The last time she was in my office, she was so rebellious that, mentally, I nearly wrote her off as one kid I wouldn't be able to help."

"She seems to have a lot of respect for you."

He sat down and thoughtfully drummed the table with his fingers.

"I don't know what's bothering her, but whatever it is, she was terribly upset when she was here."

Alex opened the paper to the sports section. "Well, if she doesn't come around to see me before school starts again, I'll call her and have her come into my office."

Robin was not sure he should wait that long to see Brenda, but Alex was sure that was best. "If I call her house and her mother answers, I'll have to tell her who it is. And if she finds out, she'll be after Brenda until she tells her why one of her teachers is trying to get in touch with her. That could be enough to blast any confidence she might have in me."

* * *

Alex and Robin Smith had almost forgotten about Brenda Ekberg's visit and the fact that she would try to see Alex some time later. When she didn't come back the afternoon following her first visit, they thought she had changed her mind or had decided to wait until school started again. Then the phone rang, and Brenda said she wanted to see him. After Alex hung up, he turned to Robin.

"Brenda seems to have the idea that she's got to see me right away."

"I'm not surprised."

He poured himself another cup of coffee and sat down at the table once more. "It may be important, but she's very capable of theatrics."

Robin shook her head. "She was terribly upset when she was here, and there was a haunted look in her eyes. She frightened me."

Alex laughed. "Brenda would enjoy hearing you say that. It would make her day if she knew she had shaken up someone."

He hadn't finished his coffee when there was a knock at the door. Robin waited until Brenda had come into their apartment before going into the living room from the kitchen.

"Hi." Brenda managed a weak little grin.

Robin spoke to her and asked her to be seated in an easy chair across from the sofa.

"I was going to wait until school started again before coming to see you, Mr. Smith," she began suddenly, "but I–I couldn't do that. I haven't been able to sleep or anything, so I decided I just had to come over and see you today."

Alex frowned. It was probably just a down slip, or an examination she had to make up. From what he understood about her from the other teachers, she was in grade trouble most of the time.

But when he spoke to her, there was no irritation in his voice. "And what is it you want to talk to me about?" he asked.

She did not answer him immediately, so he began to talk about other things – the basketball team and the state tournament Fairview was hoping to be able to play in. She seemed pleased that there was a brief measure of relief before she would have to tell him the purpose of her visit. She began to talk with artificial animation about the basketball team and about their chances for an undefeated season.

But at last, the conversation died, and Alex Smith fell silent.

"I–I–." Brenda choked on the words.

Alex leaned forward slightly to indicate that he expected her to go on.

She cleared her throat once more and began to fumble with her purse nervously. The perspiration ringed her hairline and moistened the palms of her hands.

"What seems to be the problem, Brenda." His voice was gentle and kind.

"It–It–I don't know for sure why I came to you!" The words tumbled out as though held back by a dam that had just burst. "I've hardly talked to you outside your office at school. I shouldn't be here!"

She moved as though to jump to her feet and run out of the apartment.

"Please don't go," he told her. "If you think I might be able to help you, I'd like to try. It doesn't matter whether we're in my office at school or not."

Brenda hesitated. Then she seemed to relax and settled back in the chair. "I can't talk to my mother," she said. "She'd never understand."

Alex smiled. "Your mother might surprise you by how understanding she can be, Brenda, but I know how you feel. When I was your age, I didn't think my parents understood me either."

Brenda continued, desperation gathering in her voice.

"I just had to talk to someone! I–I'm so ashamed I can't stand it anymore!"

# CHAPTER 11

# ALEX SMITH'S ADVICE

**B**renda looked from Alex Smith to his wife, Robin, and back again. Her desperation was growing. While they waited for her to continue speaking, she began to cry. First, tears welled in her eyes and clung to the tips of her long lashes. Then they began to trickle unheeded down her cheeks. Robin could stand it no longer. She got up and went over to the distraught girl, putting an arm about her thin shoulders.

That seemed to trigger her sobs. She buried her face in her hands, and her body began to shake with emotion. Robin sat on the arm of her chair and held her tenderly. She didn't say anything. The situation didn't seem to call for words. It was enough that Robin was at her side.

Alex watched helplessly. This was something they had never considered in psychology classes at the university. They talked about the release of tears and the value of crying as an emotional release, but he wasn't prepared to cope with anything like this.

Robin's heart went out to Brenda, who cried for several minutes. At last the high school girl sat up, dabbing at her eyes with a Kleenex. "I'm sorry I had to make such a scene. I didn't know this was going to be such a hang-up for me."

For the first time since Brenda started to cry, Alex spoke. "If it will help you any to tell us what this is about, we'll be glad to listen."

Her gaze met his and she managed a thin, wispy smile of appreciation. "I just had to talk to somebody – somebody who wouldn't get all up-tight and think I'm such a terrible monster!"

Robin was the one who spoke. "Nobody is going to think that of you, Brenda. As far as we're concerned, you're a teenager who has some sort of problem that we'd like to help you solve, if we can."

Alex smiled reassuringly. "A lot of people have the same sort of problems you're having."

She shook her head. "Oh, no! Nobody has done the things I've done!" Her tears threatened to start once more. "And my mother will – she'll just die if she ever finds out."

Robin took her arm away from the girl's shoulders. Sympathy at this point would only cause her to break down again, and that would serve no good purpose.

"I'm sure it's not as bad as all that." Robin spoke quietly. "Alex and I were foolish enough to run away and get married when we were in our last year of high school. I know we hurt our parents terribly, but they stayed by us. And I'm sure your mother will stay by you too. That's the way most parents are."

Brenda didn't agree with that. "But she won't!" She got up nervously and paced to the window. Then, reluctantly she turned, as though the time had finally come when she could remain silent no longer.

"You knew I went to Minneapolis for a weekend not long ago, didn't you?"

They shook their heads.

"I thought everybody knew about it. I bragged about it enough before I went and even more after I got home, but that was only to try and hide the pain I felt deep inside."

They waited in silence for her to continue.

"Somebody tried to talk me out of going." A little sob caught on the razor edge of her voice. "I should have listened to him!"

She came back and sat down, this time on a straight-backed chair some distance from Robin and Alex. And when she started to speak again, she did not look at them.

"Sandy Cole was going to go with me, but she changed her mind. She doesn't know how lucky she was! That–that was the only good thing about the whole trip!"

Robin remembered hearing something about a

trip Sandy was supposed to go on and that she had changed her mind when she gave her heart to Christ.

"That trip must have been a bitter experience."

Brenda looked up, desperation gleaming in her eyes.

"It's ruined my whole life!"

Robin and Alex glanced at each other questioningly. They had a good idea what Brenda was trying to tell them, but they couldn't be sure.

At last the girl got control of herself enough to continue talking. "I used to laugh when my mother talked to me about morals and keeping myself pure. I read about the new standards in some of the countries of Europe and here in the States and Canada. I thought free love and free sex would open up a whole new experience that my mother was too narrow-minded to understand.

"I decided it wasn't going to make any difference to me what people said. I was going to live the way *I* wanted to live. If I wanted to give myself to a boy, I was going to do it. And nothing anybody could say would stop me!"

She paused. Bitterness crept into her voice.

"Ever since I got home from Minneapolis, I have been – I haven't been able to sleep or anything. All I can think about is that awful weekend."

Robin nodded. It seemed so strange hearing this young high school girl talk about what she had done. In a way it was embarrassing, and her first reaction was to get up and go into the other room in an attempt to close out the sordidness. But, if Brenda was to be helped, the ugly affair would have to be faced. To a certain extent, it *had* to be talked about!

"Is this the reason you came to see us?" Alex asked quietly. If he was surprised by what she said, he gave no sign. His education in psychology had trained him that way.

"Partially!" She blurted out the word. "Something else has happened though. The boy I was with in Minneapolis wrote me that he's coming to Fairview to see me."

"Hmmm."

"If he does, there'll be another party like the one we had in Minneapolis and–" Her cheeks were crimson. "And it will end the same way! I don't know what to do!"

Alex looked at her helplessly. The problem, as he saw it, was to get Brenda to see that she should not have feelings of guilt over what she had done. True, it would have been much better if she had not given herself to this boy. Alex knew that some girls could not be promiscuous without causing themselves all sorts of mental and emotional problems. Brenda had probably received some Puritan teaching somewhere, sometime that had stuck with her and was causing the hang-ups.

But that really wasn't the problem of the moment, he thought. They had to face up to the fact that this boy was coming to Fairview – or that he wanted to.

In one way, the solution could be simple. She could write to the boy and inform him that she wouldn't see him. Alex had been associating with high school kids long enough, however, to know how difficult that would be for her. There was the problem of saving face – of not wanting the other kids to think she was different than they were. And, even if she did tell him not to come, there was a good chance that he and his friends would show up anyway. And if they did, there was no way of gauging the amount of pressure that would be exerted on Brenda to get her to go out with him – or what would happen if she did.

He thought he had a solution to the problem. He was sure that Robin wouldn't approve, but in his mind, she was a religious fanatic anyway. She couldn't look at this sort of thing objectively.

"This is probably going to surprise you and Robin both, Brenda," he said, "but I'm going to make a suggestion. I think you should allow the boy to come and visit you."

The girl's eyes widened.

"Are you sure that's wise, Alex?" Robin broke in.

He smiled archly. "The more I think of it, the more convinced I am that it's the only way."

Brenda considered the matter seriously. "But what do I do? Do I go out with him?"

"That's immaterial. You may want to go out with him, and yet when you see him you might not be able to stand the sound of his voice, or even being around him, because of what happened."

She shuddered. "Right now I don't think I ever want to see him again."

"I can understand that, but you've got to think of the future. You can't run from trouble continually, and you can't hide from temptation. You have to learn to rise above these things. So, before you go out with him, bring him over to talk with me, OK?"

She hesitated, frowning. "I don't think he'll come."

"He'll come, all right. But if he doesn't, we'll have to proceed without him. Having him see me isn't the key to this problem. There are other ways we can approach it."

There was a short pause.

"You've got to think high, Brenda. Keep your standards up. Learn to say, 'No,' and mean it."

When she was gone, Robin debated whether she should try to talk Alex into urging the girl to call off the date, to get her to come over to their house for the weekend, or to visit someone out of town – anything except taking a chance on seeing the boy again. She even mentioned it to him, but he disagreed firmly and that closed the matter.

"I don't want her to continue to be immoral any more than you do, but she's got to get over these feelings of guilt, and she's got to fight temptation."

All week long Alex found himself thinking about Brenda and her problem. The more he considered it, the more certain he felt that his advice was sound. He had to get the boy into his home where he could talk to him – where he could make him understand about Brenda's guilt feelings and the trouble they were causing her. As strongly as he felt about the confrontation with the boy, however, it was not until the doorbell rang early Friday evening that he was sure the youth would come. He opened the door to see a lanky, long-haired boy standing there, a superior grin on his whiskered face.

"Brenda Ekberg said I had to come and see you or no date tonight."

"Come on in." He held out his hand in a gesture of friendliness. The boy looked at it but made no move to shake hands with him.

"I don't believe I caught your name," Alex said.

"I don't believe you did either." His grin was mocking. "But my name's not going to matter one way or the other when you start talking to me, so fire away."

Alex was disturbed by the boy's attitude.

"Let's go in and sit down where we can be alone."

"What's the pitch? Are you going to give me one of those heart-to-heart talks about the birds and the bees?"

Alex fought to keep his temper under control. "I'd like to talk to you about Brenda."

The boy swaggered to a chair and sat down.

"So what do you want to know about her?"

Alex didn't like the way the conversation was going.

He had talked with all kinds of kids since he started counseling at school. He thought he had reached the place where he was shockproof. Still, he had never had anyone in his office who was so exasperating. He stood in front of the boy.

"I don't know whether you're aware of it or not, but the weekend Brenda spent with you in Minneapolis has caused her all sorts of psychological problems."

The boy squirmed uncomfortably, and his forehead flushed. "So?"

Alex had difficulty in saying exactly what he meant. He didn't want this sophisticated young man to think he was old-fashioned – a part of the Establishment. Yet he was trying to talk to him about morality and the ageless virtues.

"Brenda is so constituted mentally and emotionally that the new morality, the sexual freedom in certain circles today, creates terrible feelings of guilt – feeling so deeply rooted that they could affect her entire life."

He paused, studying his guest carefully. A sneer twisted the boy's face. "Come off it. You're putting me on."

Alex tried to continue the conversation, telling the boy how upset Brenda had been when she came to the house and what a difficult time he had had in reasoning with her. Gradually the insolence left the boy's face – or so it seemed. Finally he left, but Alex didn't know whether he had been able to get through to him or not.

* * *

Brenda Ekberg stood on the steps late Sunday night, fingers trembling as she fumbled the key into the lock. The driver of the car that she had just got out of started the engine and waved as he pulled away from the curb. She looked away quickly. She never wanted to see him again.

She was glad her mother wasn't up as she tiptoed across the living room. She couldn't face her tonight. She didn't think she could ever face anyone in Fairview again.

She didn't know what had been the matter with her. After it happened in Minneapolis, she had been so miserable she thought she would rather die than have it happen again.

But it had. And now she didn't even care whether she lived or not. She sat on the side of the bed, tears streaming down her cheeks. This wasn't what she wanted her life to be.

She left the house at the usual time the next morning, but instead of going to school she drove out onto the highway.

If only she could turn the clock back to the time she had gone out to Danny Orlis' home for that party. If only she had listened to that blind boy when he had tried to talk to her. If she had, everything would be so different for her now.

But she hadn't. And there was no way she could

wipe out what had taken place. There was no way she could erase the terrible sin in her life.

As she drove, she thought again of Alex Smith and the advice he had given her. There was no use going to see him again. He didn't have any answers for her. Still, she had to talk to somebody. Somebody who was young enough to understand and wouldn't be shocked by the way she had messed up her life.

It was then that she thought of Robin Smith. She hadn't talked to Robin much when she went to the Smith home, but Robin had been nice to her, and she acted as though she understood. At the next intersection she made a U-turn and headed back to town.

When she reached the Smith home, she was afraid to go in. She drove around the block twice before she found her nerve. When she rang the doorbell Alex opened the door.

She stared at him. "I thought you would be in school."

He laughed. "I've had a touch of the flu. So I thought I'd better stay home until noon. Is there something I can do for you?"

She shook her head. "No–I–I–."

# CHAPTER 12

# WORTH IT

**A**lex stared at her quizzically.

"I tried your advice, Mr. Smith – but it didn't help at all!"

At that moment Robin came into the living room. "I thought I heard someone at the door." She recognized the girl. "Why, hello, Brenda, how are you?"

"I–I'd like to talk to *you*, Mrs. Smith."

Alex stood aside as they went into the kitchen and closed the door. This was something he didn't understand. He was the counselor. What did Robin know about helping Brenda?

Of course, he could understand how the girl might find it easier to talk to a woman about a problem such as hers. If Robin would be sure to call him in after Brenda had talked herself out, he would be able to help the girl.

Several minutes later Robin came into the living

room. "Brenda really has a problem." There was a hushed tone in her voice. "She's so overwrought I'm afraid she might try something desperate. She might even try to do away with herself."

He got to his feet. "I'll go in and talk to her." "No." Her voice was firm.

"And just which one of us is the expert in the field of counseling?"

"I don't know anything about counseling, or about psychology either, but I do know what Brenda needs. So I've called Kay Orlis. She'll be here in 15 or 20 minutes."

Anger flecked his eyes. "Do you mean to tell me that you think making a religious fanatic out of Brenda is going to help her with her hang-ups?"

"I know that God can forgive sin."

"How naive can you get?" He snorted his indignation. "Kay Orlis! If you think religion is the answer, the least you could have done was call a preacher."

Robin did not argue with him. "I wanted to tell you that she's coming and that she'll be here soon."

He started for their bedroom but stopped and came back. "I'm going to give you a little warning, Robin. If this kid doesn't get the psychological help she needs and does take her own life, you and Kay Orlis will be responsible."

As soon as Kay arrived, Brenda began hesitantly to relate the story of the weekend in Minneapolis. She had gone to the apartment, or "pad," as she called it, where her friends lived. There were half a dozen or more boys and girls of assorted ages there.

"First, we smoked pot. I had tried it once or twice before and hadn't liked the way it made me feel, so I didn't want to do it again. But they were all trying to talk me into it, and the first thing I knew, I had taken a stick and was smoking it.

"This time the drug made me feel different than it had before. Or maybe it was just that it worked faster. I wasn't sure. Anyway, I felt this strange, exhilarating 'high,' and it seemed that anything anyone suggested was all right to do.

"Well," Brenda paused a moment, "first one couple drifted into the other room, and then another. It wasn't long until the guy I was with and I were alone."

The rest of the story fit the familiar outline of sexual immorality. She didn't have to go into any more detail. They knew well enough what had taken place.

"When I first realized what we – what I had done, I felt weak and sick inside. It was just as though I was frozen with guilt and shame."

Brenda explained how a couple of her friends had tried to talk to her the next morning. They had been living with their boyfriends for months. "We felt the same way as you do at first. It's just a normal feeling that comes because of the hang-ups our parents have given us. It'll go away after a while."

She had tried to cover up her guilt feeling by acting as casual about it as the others. When she got back to Fairview, she boasted to her friends about the wonderful time she had had that weekend. But deep inside she was writhing with shame.

"And I tried doing what Mr. Smith had told me, but it didn't do any good. It's no use trying to act as though it doesn't matter what I do. I feel as though I've ruined my whole life." A stifled sob punctuated her words.

Kay Orlis listened quietly, but she did not act shocked at what Brenda had told her. That wouldn't help the overwrought girl. Besides, both she and Danny had seen much of the sordidness and sin of the world, even though they hadn't indulged in it. When she spoke, her voice was quiet, but it was firm and controlled.

"It is true that you've committed a terrible sin, Brenda. And, I suppose, in a way, it is a sin that will scar you for the rest of your life. There are some sins that are that way."

The girl started to cry once more. Kay did not go on until she had stopped and wiped her eyes.

"As I said, this is a terrible, scarring sin that often leaves its mark. I wouldn't be honest if I didn't level with you about that. But it doesn't have to ruin your life. You can rise above what happened."

"That's what Mr. Smith told me, but it didn't work."

Kay opened her purse, took out her Bible, and read the story of David and Bathsheba.

"Don't forget that David was a fine man – a king

– but he was tempted, and he committed the same kind of sin. And after he had sinned, he made it even worse by sending the woman's husband off to fight a battle in a place where he was sure to be killed."

Brenda shuddered.

"God punished David for his sin, but when David repented, God forgave him."

Hope flickered in Brenda's eyes. "Do–do you suppose God would forgive me?"

"Of course He will. He tells us in the Bible that He will forgive all our sins. 'Though your sins be as scarlet, they shall be as white as snow.' "

Brenda listened, incredulous. She had supposed there could be no forgiveness for what she had done, but Kay was so positive, she began to take heart herself.

Kay Orlis quoted the words of Jesus, "the one who comes to Me I will certainly not cast out."

"But next to murder, it's the worst thing a person can do!" Brenda blurted.

"That's not true," Kay told her. "The worst sin you've committed is the same sin I committed before giving my heart and life to Christ. It's the same sin that DeeDee and Sandy and everyone else has committed. That sin is rebellion against God."

Brenda wrinkled her forehead questioningly.

"When we rebel against God, we deliberately choose to follow Satan. You see, it was your rebellion against God that caused you to commit this sin and all the rest of the sins in your life."

Tears came back to Brenda's eyes.

"But, if you decide that you're not going to rebel against God anymore, and if you receive Him as your Savior, He will blot out all your sin."

She paused to give Brenda time to think about what she had just told her. It was a minute or more before she continued. "If you want to be forgiven, the Lord will forgive you," she said, her voice quiet. "But if you don't, He won't force it on you. You have to make the choice."

"Oh, I want it!" The words burst from Brenda's lips.

Kay studied the girl's serious, young face briefly. Brenda seemed to be sincere, as much so as anyone she had ever talked with, but there was something about her that caused Kay to hesitate. She opened the Bible to a number of other verses, explaining in different ways what it would mean to Brenda if she turned her life over to Christ.

"It must be more than just being sorry for this particular sin you have committed. You've got to be sorry enough to want a new life, to put all your old life behind you, and to live the way God would have you to live, with His help."

For the first time doubt crept into Brenda's eyes. "I don't know whether I can do that or not," she murmured.

"You can't do it in your own strength. Neither can I, nor anyone else. God says He will help you. But you have to want to be different than you are – completely different."

Brenda frowned. "What do you mean?"

Kay searched for words. "I think I can explain it best in this way. So often we want what God has to give us, but we don't want to give Him anything in return. He's not satisfied with that. He not only wants to be our Savior, but He also wants to be the Lord of our lives as well."

Brenda squirmed uneasily in her chair. "I thought–" her voice trailed off into silence.

"You see," Kay went on, "God knows that we can't direct our lives ourselves and live in a way that will be pleasing to Him. He wants us to yield completely to Him, to let Him do exactly as He wishes with us."

"But–." The word popped out.

"But what, Brenda?"

Her manner seemed to change slightly. Her voice firmed and she sat up straight.

"Nothing."

There was a long pause before Kay continued. "Too many of us want God to take away the sin that is causing us problems and making us feel guilty, but there are certain areas of our lives that we're not willing to let Him have. We can't bargain with Him."

Brenda's gaze met hers. "But I–I'd lose all my friends and–and everything."

Kay nodded. "You might lose all your friends, that's true."

The silence was agonizing.

"I couldn't *stand* that!"

Kay breathed deeply. "God would give you new friends – even better and truer friends than you have now, but you must be willing to *trust* Him."

"I had no idea it would be so hard. I thought–."

"In a way it's so easy. All you have to do is turn yourself completely over to God and let Him give you a new life."

Brenda hesitated. "I–I'll have to think about it."

Tears came to Kay's eyes. "Don't wait too long, Brenda."

There were tears in Brenda's eyes too as she thanked Kay and Robin and hurried out, but she was able to hold them in check until she reached the car. There she rested her head on the steering wheel and began to sob.

She wanted forgiveness for what she had done. She wanted to live a clean, honorable life, but the price was so high – so very high! Was it worth it?

Brenda started the car and drove aimlessly for a time, thinking. She wondered what life might be like without her old friends. Would she really miss them? And what was it Kay had said about God's giving her a new life? Maybe that *would* be better than the agony she was going through now.

A new look of determination and hope etched her tear-stained face as she turned in the direction of the Orlis home. Maybe Kay was right. Perhaps it *was* worth it.

# THE
# DANNY ORLIS
# SERIES

The Danny Orlis series, by Bernard Palmer, delivers a blend of adventure, mystery, and suspense through various settings—from the Canadian wilderness to Guatemalan jungles. Danny Orlis, an adept outdoorsman, skilled athlete, and committed Christian, employs his quick thinking, calm bravery, and biblical solutions to confront everyday problems and hair-raising dangers. Early stories focus on Danny navigating school life, sports, and outdoor challenges, while in later books, Danny and his wife Kay provide wisdom and guidance to youngsters facing lifelike situations and challenges. Having sold over two million copies, this series has made Palmer a renowned author in Christian youth literature. Palmer is also the author of the Felicia Cartright series and various other series for Christian youth.

## AVAILABLE FROM WWW.ANEKOPRESS.COM

www.ingramcontent.com/pod-product-compliance
Lightning Source LLC
Chambersburg PA
CBHW060501300726
48975CB00008B/2599